Get Croc'd Before "I Do"

A Simone Simpson Mystery

Rita Smircich

Get Croc'd Before "I Do"

A Simone Simpson Mystery

Rita Smircich

Published by "I Do" LLC

Cover design by Chris Murphy: www.cmurph.com
Book design by Pamela Pitcher: pam@documentclarity.com

Paperback ISBN: 978-1-7335014-3-9
First Edition

Printed in the United States of America 2021

Thank you to the "I Do" Team. Without their help and expertise, these books would not be possible.

Judith Marks-White, author, teacher, editor, and friend for her continued encouragement and support. I can't thank her enough for all the hours she dedicated to my craft. She kept me going through good and difficult times, and knocked the writer's block off my head numerous times.

Chris Murphy, Illustrator, for his continued patience and creative mind. I don't know how he does it, but all I need to tell him are a few simple facts, and he creates incredible book covers time and time again.

To Ed Kelly, my life partner, for his love, laughs, hope and input. Special thanks for taking this journey with me, and for lifting me up every time I said I can't go on.

To Pamela Pitcher, Layout and Design and "sushi sister" for her creative vision, incredible patience, and continuous laughter.

To Laurie Goldberg, proofreader, computer wizard, friend, fellow kitchen witch, confidant . . . the list goes on. Thank you for the continuous hand-holding and tolerance.

Special thanks to:
Frank Mazzotti, Ph.D. a/k/a "The Croc Doc"
Professor, University of Florida

Dedicated to the millions of lives lost to COVID-19.

Memories and love to Dr. Joseph Tamagna, a long-time friend. Your loss is beyond words. Know that you were, and still are, loved by so many you've left behind.

Other books by Rita Smircich:

To Do Before "I Do"
Advice, Wisdom & Practical Ideas for
Organizing and Planning Your Wedding

I Killed Grandma in Utero

Simone Simpson Mystery Series:
Die Before "I Do"
See Paris Before "I Do"
Drown Before "I Do"

Simone Simpson series books and Kindle
are available through Amazon.com

Introduction

December 31, 2019

Grand Hamilton Hotel Banquet Hall

Greenwich, Connecticut

11:30 PM

Simone Simpson mingled among the guests at the annual Grand Hamilton Hotel's New Year's Eve celebration, observing those who were consuming more alcohol that was necessary. Inebriated women fawned on acquaintances, while their spouses ignored the flirtations. The noise level rose in rhythm with the merriment and the music. This was "the event of the year" where reporters from local and national newspapers, and tabloids, gathered fodder. Gossip columnists, noted the important "who's who," the suspected and imagined affairs, the latest designer dresses and suits, and who displayed the largest and most opulent blinding diamonds. Revelry abounded. Laughter, air kisses and champagne flowed freely.

Simone noticed several suited gentlemen off in the corner engrossed in deep conversation, oblivious to the gaiety only several feet away from them. All were government officials, from a former FBI agent, to the governor of the state, to the town's mayor.

Attendance at this annual event had grown over time. This year's six-hundred-fifty guests pushed the hotel to its maximum capacity. At $1,500 a plate, the hotel would be able to cover their costs, plus some profit that would be donated to a charitable organization. Each year the hotel chose a charity focusing on helping people starting their life over, due to some tragic event such as a home fire, job loss or a similar catastrophe. "A new year, a new beginning," was their motto.

Charlie Hamilton, Simone's husband, snuck up behind her and placed his arms around her waist. "You look ravishing, my love," he whispered in her ear. "I love you so much."

Simone turned to face her husband; her eyes similarly transmitting her feelings. Her love for him was never so profoundly resonant as it was at that moment. They kissed, tenderly.

"Did you notice the group of G-men?" Simone whispered.

"I did," Charlie said. "They were talking about a SARS-like virus in China that was spreading quickly. Some diplomats were being called back home. There's a concern the virus might spread to the United States. That's all I heard before they caught me eavesdropping. They quickly changed the subject."

"They've been huddled together for quite a while," Simone said. "I wish they'd discuss these matters outside of a festive gathering. I'm sure the distance from their loved ones is causing some concern, angst, and possibly even random rumors."

Suddenly, the music stopped. The MC announced, "Ten . . . nine . . . eight . . ."

Simone and Charlie turned to face the stage. From behind the band, ceiling to floor drapery swiftly parted. The audience was transported to Times Square where a multi-ton Waterford crystal-covered ball was making its way to the ground. Cheers, hoots and hollers reverberated throughout the ballroom.

"Three . . . two . . . one! Happy New Year!"

Suddenly, hundreds of silver balloons were released from their ceiling netting, raining over all. At the same time, strategically positioned employees shot guns of confetti into the air. A fresh roar of cheers ensued. People embraced one another with their glasses filled with tiny pieces of colorful shreds of paper.

Simone observed the crowd. People were celebrating as if life was devoid of any restrictions, fear and doom that might possibility arrive. She glanced over at the group engrossed in their personal conversation. A woman approached them and tugged on the arm of one of the men, seemingly annoyed that she had been left alone and ignored, and was not being appropriately kissed at the stroke of midnight. The man succumbed to her wishes and joined her. The group quickly dispersed, and they went in search of their respective partners.

Simone whispered to Charlie, "I wonder if they suspect something ominous is brewing that could even be a national threat. I'm worried about our babies . . . our friends and family . . . our safety . . .

Her fears were consoled by her husband, "Don't worry, my love," Charlie tried assuring her, while his own concerns took hold. "Don't worry."

$\mathcal{O}ne$

Eleven Months Earlier

Westport, Connecticut

February 2019

On an unusually warm February Saturday afternoon, Simone's neighbor Cynthia, while walking her dog, noticed Charlie and Simone sitting on their deck reading the newspaper. She asked if she could speak with them.

Her dog, Grendel, was a one-hundred-pound Rottweiler, known by the neighbors as the sweetest and most affectionate gentle giant in the neighborhood. He licked the couple's hands while energetically wagging his stub of a tail. He plopped down on the deck, emitting an exhausted grunt.

After pleasantries were exchanged, Cynthia blurted out, "I wanted to tell you that Brett and I are going to sell our home and move to North Carolina. Brett's company is moving its headquarters to Raleigh, and since he's their top litigation attorney on tech, they made him a fantastic offer."

Cynthia had been the first person to welcome Simone to Westport. She had introduced Simone to the contractor who did all the renovations and home improvements.

"When are you moving?" Charlie asked.

"We're thinking of putting the house on the market in early April, and hope it sells before the summer. We're going down next weekend to look at the area, and see what our options are. Brett's job starts in March, so he'll have to commute until then. I'm going to hate leaving Westport," Cynthia said, her voice trailing off. "We're hoping to sell the furniture as my beachy décor won't work down south. If we can hang in there for a decade or so, we'll move to Florida."

"I'm going to miss you," Simone said as she reached for her neighbor's hand. Grendel's ears perked up. The dog was extremely protective, and was at the quick if he sensed any danger. Cynthia looked at Grendel and whispered, "It's okay." The dog settled back down and yawned.

"We'll miss you too, Simone. If you know of anyone who might be interested in buying the house, let me know."

Simone said she might know someone, and she'd get back to her if there was any interest.

After Cynthia and Grendel left, Charlie asked his wife who the interested party might be. Simone's smile stretched across her face. Charlie immediately knew the answer.

Simone was an astute business woman, and was quick to jump on an opportunity that would be in her favor. On Monday morning, she contacted her attorney, Sidney Harding.

"Hi Sid. It's Simone. I need you to authorize a purchase."

Over the years, Simone had inherited a substantial settlement from her deceased husband's accident and her parents' passing. In addition to her successful wedding planning business, she had amassed an estate of over $15 million. Now, years later, it had grown to well over $25 million. Her wealth was kept secret, even from her business partner, Jennifer Keys. Only a select few, like the Smith family, Charlie, and her accountant and attorney, knew how much money Simone actually had in the bank.

She was frugal, but when she wanted something, she didn't hesitate to purchase it. And she wanted Cynthia's house before anyone else had a chance to scoop it out from under her.

Sidney informed Simone that the money, held in a managed trust, would be released after an official request was presented to the Trustees. He assured Simone that the request would not face any difficulties, as she rarely asked for any funds. In fact, her annual allowance of $75,000 was never taken; it remained in the trust to earn growth.

"I want the purchase to be made through an LLC. My name has to stay out of it for as long as possible. I haven't decided if I want the sellers to know who bought their house. Can you do that?"

"I'm sure that won't be a problem, Simone." Sidney promised he would get back to her within a week.

Three weeks later, Cynthia received a registered letter with the official offer. She ran to Simone's house, charged up the stairs, and banged on her front door. She could hardly contain her excitement.

"Simone! Simone! Are you home?"

"One minute," Simone shouted at the door. She padded her way to the front door. Cynthia stood there; her face flushed with enthusiasm. She wasn't wearing a winter coat, gloves, or any protection against the harsh wind blowing off the water. When Simone saw her neighbor's face, she was frightened at first, thinking something awful had happened to her husband or son.

"What is it, Cynthia? Are you okay? Do you need the police . . . fire . . . is someone following you?"

"No," Cynthia assured her. "Nothing like that." She paused to take a breath. "I've got some incredible news, and I want you to be the first to hear it."

"Come in from the cold," Simone said. "Tell me what happened while I brew some tea."

But Cynthia could not hold back. "Someone made an all-cash offer of $875,000 for our home. Sight unseen . . . slightly above market value. It's a direct offer. It came from our attorney."

"What?" shouted Simone, incredulously. "How, or should I say, when did this happen? It sounds fishy to me." Simone was enjoying this game and was surprised at how well she was able to play the innocent neighbor. She turned her back on Cynthia to finish preparing the Roobios tea, and to avoid her from seeing the wide grin on her face.

"And," Cynthia added, "They want to pay an additional $125,000 for all the possessions. Everything -- including the furniture, fully stocked cupboards: dishes, glassware, pots, pans, bedding, and area carpets . . . right down to a container of fat-free milk in the fridge."

"Are you making this up?" Simone said acting coy, as she took the agreement from Cynthia's hand. "Who would do this? I thought you weren't going to put the house on the market until April. Does Brett know?"

"No, you're the first person I've told. I can't contain myself. It's as if someone was listening in on our family's conversations about starting fresh, with new furniture in a new location. Simone, this is too good to be true."

"You know what they say: 'If it sounds too good to be true, it usually is.' What did your attorney say? I assume he's the one who sent you this agreement."

"He said he has to do some due diligence to see if this is a real offer, and not some prank. Apparently, the buyers don't want their identity known. Look at the purchaser's name: CASH LLC. Yes, the offer is all cash, but do they have to shove it in my face that they're rich?"

Simone acted as if she was seeing this document for the very first time. "That is a strange name for a company," Simone agreed.

"My attorney thinks it might be a TV celebrity, or a rich hedge-fund guy who doesn't want anyone knowing he's buying a place in Westport. Oh Simone, this is so exciting," Cynthia gushed. "I can't wait to tell Brett when he comes home tonight. He's going to faint."

The two women sat at Simone's kitchen table while they sipped cups of herbal tea and nibbled at buttery

English biscuits. They discussed Cynthia's plans, and fears about moving to Raleigh.

"I'm afraid of being so far away from the water, Simone," Cynthia said, as she stared out of Simone's expansive living room picture window facing Long Island Sound. "We're looking at homes in Cary, North Carolina. There are some new homes being built in fifty-five plus developments. When Brett is at work, I'll get to meet the neighbors at the club house. Maybe I'll learn how to play mahjong, or pickle ball," Cynthia joked. She quickly added, "You and Charlie – and the babies – must visit after we get settled."

"We will. We are planning to visit Mrs. Smith in the early fall, and Raleigh is only a few hours away from Charlottesville. I'm going to miss you, my friend. I'll never forgot how hospitable you and your family were after I purchased this house, known by the locals as the Old Raymo House. And, I'll never forget how you fixed me up with Pete Cody, the contractor."

Cynthia lowered her voice, as if the embryos, in uteri, could hear her, and she whispered, "Does Charlie know about Pete?"

"He knows there was another man in my life before him. But that was in the past, and best to leave it there. I'm happy Pete reconnected with Joyce, and has been blessed with a large family. I just couldn't give him what he wanted; not at the time."

Cynthia sat staring into her mug, as if looking for an answer among the tea leaves. After a few moments of silence, she asked, "Who would want to buy my house, sight unseen, with all the contents? It doesn't make sense, Simone. I have a gut feeling it's being purchased by someone I know. Someone who knows we are moving to North Carolina, and has seen the inside of my home. I don't think anyone would spend that kind of money on a house they never set foot in."

"It's the location, Cynthia," Simone assured her. "And, if anyone peeked in your windows, they'd see you have fabulous taste. I'm sure they did a Google Earth search, saw it was on the Gold Coast of Westport, and decided they wanted to be close to the beach."

"But how did they know we were going to put the house on the market?" She looked at Simone, her eyes wide. "I hope our real estate agent isn't going to be angry we're not listing it with her. Oh, my, Simone, do you think she'll sue us for a commission?"

"Did you sign a listing agreement with her?"

"No, not yet."

"Then, you don't have any obligation. If you'd like to appease her, give her a substantial gift certificate, like a weekend away at Canyon Ranch, or a long weekend in the Caribbean."

"You always know the answers to every problem, Simone."

"I try," Simone buried her smiling face in her cup of tea.

"I still don't know how anyone found out. Maybe the real estate agent told the others in her office, and someone went behind her back."

"I doubt that would happen," Simone assured. "Most agents keep future listings close to their chest. But people do talk, Cynthia. You know that. Maybe you casually mentioned it at one of your dinner parties. Or, perhaps someone in Brett's office passed it on. Word gets out very quickly when a home as beautiful as yours is coming on the market." She looked at her friend, trusting she was buying into her story. "I hope we get nice neighbors," Simone continued, "and not someone who jets in for the weekend, and has loud late-night parties. After all, I will have two little ones who will require lots of sleep." Simone said as she rubbed her extended belly.

"Yeah, I guess word does get around. Sometimes I think men are worse gossipers than women. I wouldn't put it past the lawyers in Brett's office to tell their associates on the West Coast. I wonder if someone in Brett's office can break through the purchaser's secret identity. Lawyers have access to all sorts of information."

Simone's face suddenly grew pale. She had forgotten that Brett had access to databases the average person didn't.

Cynthia noticed the change in Simone's appearance. "Are you okay, Simone? You look ashen."

"I'm fine. Just tired. I usually nap at this time," she said looking at the kitchen clock.

"Oh, Simone, I'm sorry I took up so much of your time," Cynthia said, as she headed towards the front door.

"It's late. I've got to start dinner. I'll call you later after I tell Brett the news."

The women stood at the threshold to Simone's home, and hugged over Simone's extended belly. Simone felt guilty for not telling Cynthia she was the purchaser of the home, hiding behind an LLC, but the timing wasn't right. Possibly, after the closing.

She closed the door behind Cynthia, sat down on the sofa, and propped her legs up on the coffee table. She recalled the first time she broached the subject to Mrs. Virginia Smith and Irene about being the twin's nannies.

"Oh, you're so sweet, Simone, but Irene and I are happy here in our home in the hills. Besides, who would take care of our house? No, I couldn't accept your offer,"

"Think about it, Mrs. Smith," Simone begged. *"Discuss the idea with your daughter and future son-in-law. I need you in my life, once again. After all Mrs. Smith, these are your grandchildren."* The older woman was touched by this sentiment.

"I know it'd be a big sacrifice to move from the hills of Virginia to the beach of New England, but a change might be the best thing for you." Simone hesitated a moment, then added, *"You could rent out your house to a University of Virginia professor. I'm sure Judy or Harold, being teachers, can help find a family."*

"I'll discuss it with my daughter, Simone, but I think I know the answer. I'm sure you could hire a nanny from a reputable company. I just don't think at my age I'd be of any help."

Simone knew that at sixty-eight, Mrs. Smith, with the help of Irene, had all the energy and ability to help with the twins by working side by side. Besides, if after six months it wasn't working for either family, they could return to Virginia. Simone would have no difficulty renting out the property during the summer, enough to pay the real estate taxes, maintenance and insurance. This was a golden opportunity for Mrs. Smith and Irene to move to Westport. Granted, it was a selfish wish, and Simone knew that. Yet, she couldn't think of anyone else she'd want to help raise the newborns. Her thoughts drifted, and within minutes she was asleep.

Charlie arrived an hour later and found his wife napping. He unpacked the dinner he picked up from DaPietro's, set the table, and poured himself a scotch. The soft classical music from the Amazon Echo awoke Simone. She smiled at her husband, who watched her while she arose.

"Hello, my love. Did you have a good day?" he asked.

She simply said, "Cynthia received the offer."

Two

May 18, 2019

Charlottesville, Virginia

"I, Judy, take you, Harold, to be my wedded husband. To have and to hold, from this day forward, for better, for worse, for richer, for poorer . . ."

Simone, matron-of-honor for her best friend, Judy Smith, listened as the couple exchanged vows. She glanced at Mrs. Smith who dabbed at her tear-filled eyes as she listened to her daughter's words. Simone looked across the way and focused on the best man, her husband, Charlie. They locked eyes. His smile beamed as he looked at his beautiful wife and her protruding stomach, housing their soon-to-be twins.

Suddenly, intense emotions washed over Simone. She attributed these to being pregnant, in need of a ladies' room, and pulsating swollen ankles. Simone tried to refocus on the ceremony, but her mind ticked away the seconds until she could waddle down the aisle and charge directly into a bathroom stall.

Simone's staff at "I Do" LLC were the event planners for Judy and Harold's wedding, overseeing every detail. The May wedding was held on the Smith family's estate in Charlottesville, Virginia. The bride was surprisingly relaxed, a sense of calm emanating on her face. The weather was perfect, with a soft breeze off the mountains and high cumulus clouds. The bride's strapless, tea-length dress featured an A-Line style. Delicate translucent beads sparkled in the sunlight as she walked across the lawn. Her neck was graced with a simple solitaire diamond necklace, and stud earrings to match. Judy never required much makeup, and today was no exception. She was strikingly beautiful au naturel.

The wedding ceremony was held outdoors, under an enormous weeping willow that Judy once climbed as a child. There, her father had built a tree house which became her favorite hideaway where she played Nancy Drew: Girl Detective with school friends. On her perch she spied on the adults as they danced and drank during the elegant dinners her parents hosted.

Now, only memories remained of the wooden structure. During the ceremony, Judy looked up to where the clubhouse once stood and whispered a heartfelt 'thank you' to her deceased father.

The couple chose lavender as their wedding theme, the tablecloths displaying a kiss of the color. The napkins were white, and the centerpieces, which at 30" high, were filled with white roses, dark purple and cascading complimentary flowers. As a memento, guests were gifted with a six-ounce flacon of fragrant essential floral oil, wrapped in natural raffia, with a sprig of baby's breath.

"The wedding was perfect," gushed Judy to Simone at the end of the evening. "My only regret was not having my father here. I know my mother missed him as well."

Simone tried to hug her friend, but her enormous belly intervened, allowing only hand holding and air kisses. They giggled at the awkwardness of the moment.

"He was here, Judy. I could feel him looking down on you and Harold, giving his blessings. I miss him, too." At this affirmation, Simone burst into tears. The last few months had been emotional, with so many changes happening in her life and the lives of the people around her. Soon, she'd be a mother to twins. She didn't have any family, other than the Smiths', and an estranged brother who lived in Kentucky. Simone resided in Connecticut, and Mrs. Smith lived in Virginia, hundreds of miles apart. Simone feared she'd fail as a new mother, and begged Mrs. Smith to move to Westport to help her, especially during the first several months. Simone researched, and had at the ready, a lactation consultant, a night nurse, and a nanny ready to jump in. But her deep desire was to have Mrs. Smith and her housekeeper, Irene, living close by to do the job instead of all these strangers.

"Oh, Simone, don't cry," begged Judy.

"It's the hormones . . . and my fat ankles. I'm sorry," Simone apologized. "I don't think I'll ever get my figure back . . . what if I drop one of the babies . . . what if I get them mixed up . . ."

Judy said sternly, "Look at me, Simone."

Simone wiped away her tears complying with her friend's demand.

"SOAP!"

Simone burst into laughter, joined by her best friend. "You're right, Judy. I must remember our secret code: SOAP. Stop Obsessing About Possibilities."

When the two were college roommates, they constantly reminded each other of this acronym. Either they obsessed over tests, boys or their part-time jobs. At such moments, they supported each other with only one word: "SOAP!"

"The wedding was so beautiful," Simone said.

"Thanks to you, and your staff," Judy agreed. "Between Harold and I working, helping mom and planning a wedding I could never have pulled this off. No, Simone, we could have never planned a more perfect day. We are so pleased."

"When are you leaving for your honeymoon?" Simone asked.

"Not for a while. Harold still has final papers to grade. When we are both finished with school, we'll take a week off. We are thinking of a small cabin in the Blue Ridge Mountains, far enough away from Richmond, but not too far from mom in case she needs us."

"Judy, I really hope your mom and Irene agree to move next door to Charlie and me. She'd be such a huge help, and we can watch over her, instead of you and Harold always running between Richmond and Charlottesville."

"Don't worry, Simone, I've been trying to convince her that idea would be a great adventure, and she'd be helping you. Please don't tell mom, but Harold's been offered a position at a college in Massachusetts."

"Oh my," Simone shouted, a little too loudly. She lowered her voice, "That'd be great. You'd be even closer to me."

"We were discussing the pros and cons. I'd have to get my Massachusetts' teaching license to get a job up there, though I'd lose the years I've put in here. It's a lot to think about. I don't want to say anything to mom. Harold said he's going to put off giving them an answer until he knows what she's going to do. We don't want to leave her here, alone, while we are all up in the northeast."

"What a guy . . . I mean, husband," Simone said, giggling.

Their nervous laughter marked the end of a stressful day and a stressful time for them both.

"Oops!" Simone said suddenly. "I need a ladies' room. I've discovered my bladder can't handle too much laughter."

As she waddled off, she blew a kiss at her best friend, who was more like the sister she never had.

Three

All that was left to complete Simone's scheme was to convince Mrs. Smith, along with her housekeeper, Irene, to move into Cynthia's home, and become caretakers to the twins and assist in raising them.

Mrs. Smith had taken Simone in during her college years after Simone's parents were killed in an automobile accident. After college, Simone had married Joe Simpson. Hours after she learned she was carrying their child, they were struck down by a speeding taxi in New York City. Joe died in her arms. She lost the baby in the accident, and suffered several broken bones. She never thought she'd be able to carry a child again, let alone twins.

After the accident, Henry and Virginia Smith helped Simone clean out her Tribeca apartment. She moved to the Smiths' farmhouse in Charlottesville, Virginia, where they supported Simone during her first years of widowhood while she recovered. After three years of their loving support, Judy and Simone traveled to an event planner's conference, where Simone met Jennifer Keys. Simone and Jennifer became fast friends, and within a short time, Simone opened "I Do" LLC in Fairfield, Connecticut, with Jennifer as her business partner.

Now Simone juggled her life as a wife, a soon-to-be mother, and a business owner. During Simone's maternity leave, the plan was for Jennifer to oversee the office operations, and keep Simone updated. The last piece of the puzzle was for Mrs. Smith to accept her generous but unusual offer.

Simone's phone rang. When she saw the caller i.d., her heart skipped a beat.

"Hello, Mrs. Smith," Simone said, forcing herself to stay in control. "How are you and Irene?"

Mrs. Smith responded with a lift in her voice. "Irene and I were just talking about you this morning over breakfast."

Please say yes. Please say yes, Simone prayed to herself.

"Irene and I discussed moving to Westport, and have come to a decision."

"Yes?" Simone said as she prayed her silent prayer again.

"We'd be honored to accept your offer, and be 'pseudo-grandmothers' to the babies."

Simone was lost for words, which rarely occurred. Without warning, she burst into tears, sobbing into the phone, "Oh, Mrs. Smith. You have no idea what this means to us."

"Now, now Simone. Please calm down. After all, we don't want these babies arriving early because you're an emotional wreck," she chuckled.

"Yes, of course. It seems these days I cry at everything. Yesterday I found myself crying over some sappy TV commercial."

"It's the hormones, dear," assured the experienced older woman. "It will pass. Soon you won't have time for tears. You'll be too busy running in circles."

Simone smiled.

"Just give us some time to gather our belongings. Judy and Harold are coming this weekend and will help us pack. They're equally excited that I'll be next door to you, especially since they live over an hour away from here. We hope to arrive in Westport shortly before or after the twins are born."

Simone proceeded to update Mrs. Smith on the purchase of Cynthia's home. She explained how the house would be purchased under an LLC, so that her and Charlie's name would not be noted in the contract. "I'm planning to keep my name a secret."

"Do you think that's a good idea?" Mrs. Smith inquired. "After all, she *is* a friend and a good neighbor. She's certainly going to find out sooner or later, especially after Irene and I move into the house. The neighbors will talk, and Cynthia might feel insulted that you didn't trust her enough to tell her you are the buyer."

"A very good point. I didn't think about the consequences. I'll discuss it with Charlie this evening. Maybe we'll have Cynthia and Brett over for dinner this weekend, and reveal our secret identity. Charlie will know what to say. My mind is somewhat muddled these days, what with the babies coming soon, plus work. I feel blessed to have Jennifer and my great staff running things for me."

"I'm sorry we can't be there sooner, Simone, but it's just impossible."

"Not to worry. We've hired a doula to help during the first couple of weeks; until you get here." Simone was quiet for a moment. "I love you very much, Mrs. Smith. You're more of a mother to me than my own mother was. She was controlled by my father . . . she never got to meet you or Mr. Smith . . . or Irene . . . she was . . ."

Simone blabbered on until the voice on the other end said, "I love you too, Simone, and I look forward to this new adventure. I admit that it was a big decision to move from the hills of Virginia to the beach in Connecticut. Irene was apprehensive, too, but I finally convinced her."

The women ended their conversation, just as Charlie walked through the door.

"Hello, my love," he said, giving his wife a kiss.

Four

Friday evening came sooner than expected. There was so much to do before the babies arrived, setting up the nursery, ordering furniture, planning an informal baby shower organized by Jennifer. The days seemed to flow into weeks.

Simone walked around her house and practiced what she was going to say to Cynthia and Brett. Maybe she should have waited another week, but then she might be tied up with doctors' appointments, or work, or the babies if they arrived early. No, Mrs. Smith was right. It was important for her neighbors to know now that she was the new homeowner.

The men talked about business while Charlie poked at the fireplace logs. Simone and Cynthia chatted about the nursery.

"You're awfully quiet this evening," Cynthia said as she tore the lettuce leaves. "Are you feeling okay? Maybe we should do this another night?"

"Oh, I'm fine, Cynthia. There's just a lot going on at the office, with two big weddings coming up and planning for the arrival of the babies." Simone removed a large tray of baked ziti from the oven, compliments of her housekeeper, Anna Maria.

Dinner was delicious, but the conversations were disjointed, and seemed almost forced. The four usually talked over each other, with so much to share and discuss. This evening seemed strained, with tension between them. Finally, over an assortment of Italian pastries and cappuccinos, Simone made her move.

"Cynthia and Brett," Simone said, "Charlie and I have something to tell you. We're not sure how you're going to take it."

"Is something wrong with the babies, Simone? You've been so distant . . . quiet . . . I sensed something was wrong." Cynthia exchanged glances between them and said, "Please tell us you're all right."

"Dear," Brett interrupted his wife. "Let Simone speak."

"I feel we owe you an apology," Simone said, "Charlie and I have been a bit sneaky."

"What do you mean?" Cynthia asked, seemingly confused.

Simone smiled at her friend. "When you came to my house excited about selling the house, I wanted to tell you something I felt you needed to know."

Cynthia placed her teacup on the table, sat back, and waited for the news. Perhaps, she thought, Simone and Charlie were also moving. Several scenarios ran through her mind. She never expected what came next.

"Charlie and Simone Hamilton," said Simone looking at her neighbors.

Cynthia and Brett looked confused.

"Yeah, so," Brett said after a few uncomfortable moments.

Simone repeated the phrase, but it still fell on deaf ears. "CASH," said Simone. Charlie and I are CASH LLC. We are purchasing your home."

Silence ensued. No one said a word. Cynthia's mouth dropped open, and Brett's eyes were dark and unemotional.

Finally, the reality settled in, and it was apparent that Brett did not take the news as well as the couple expected. He placed his napkin on the table, pushed his chair back, and walked to the kitchen sink filling a glass with water. He mumbled softly, "Of all the underhanded things."

Simone's eyes filled, but no tears flowed this time. She was embarrassed more than shocked by her neighbor's reaction.

Brett walked back to the table and sat down. He was visibly angry. "Why didn't you just tell us that you wanted to buy our house, instead of playing this charade?"

"Because Brett," Charlie answered, "we don't believe in doing business with family and friends. I've been burned in the past. Besides, we doubted you would have sold us the house at market value. This way, you two can start a new life down south, knowing your home was sold to people who will take care of it, and love it as much as you have."

"Are you planning to move into it, Simone?" Cynthia asked. "What will you do with this house?" She was about to go off on a litany of additional questions, but Brett put his hand on hers, a sign to stop.

"We plan to move Mrs. Smith and Irene into the house to become nannies to our babies," said Simone.

Cynthia got up from her chair and ran to hug her neighbors. "Oh, that's lovely."

"Well, I don't think it's so lovely," said Brett angrily. "I still think you hid behind a cloak of deceit."

Charlie spoke up. "Brett, do you feel you were duped? Did we cheat you out of your home, your possessions? Are we forcing you to move? Did we insult you by making a low-ball offer? Did we demand immediate possession? All you had to do was reject the offer. You can put the house on the market in a few months, or next year, and work with your realtor." Charlie's tone was level, but firm.

Brett suddenly realized he was acting like an ungracious fool. Instead, he should be thankful his home was being purchased by a wonderful couple. He and his wife wouldn't have to deal with open houses, negotiations, unqualified buyers trying to low ball them, or people traipsing through. Instead, he should be thanking Charlie and Simone for what they did.

"I'm sorry," Brett said sheepishly. "I was very suspicious of the offer. But now that you've explained it to us, we are grateful for your generous and gracious offer. But all cash, Charlie?"

Simone reached over and put her finger up against Brett's lips, and said, "The less questions asked, the better."

The remainder of the evening flowed as if nothing had happened between the two couples. Brett and Charlie migrated to the bar for snifters of brandy, while the women cleaned up the dishes. It seemed like old times with easy and relaxed conversations.

"When do you think Mrs. Smith and Irene will arrive?" Cynthia asked.

"I'm hoping before the babies come in August," Simone said. "But, that's not to say, you need to move out on my account," she quickly added. "The women can stay with us until the house is ready."

"I'm thrilled that you and Charlie are buying our home. I know it'll be well taken care of. I'm going to miss you so much, my friend."

"And, I will miss you, Cynthia." The two women hugged. "Before we become weepy rag dolls, let's join the men."

The evening concluded after midnight. Simone couldn't wait to climb into bed. Her ankles were swollen, and the slightest pounding of a headache was beginning.

One month later, Simone hosted a going-away party for the family, attended by neighbors and friends. Many tears were shed that day.

"I'll call when we arrive, Simone. I only wish we could be here for the birth of the babies," Cynthia said as she hugged Simone goodbye.

"I'll send photos, I promise," Simone said.

One day after the over-sized moving van drove away, Simone's housekeeper did a deep cleaning of the home, and stocked the cupboards and refrigerator with essentials. All Mrs. Smith and Irene had to do was bring their clothes and personal effects.

Five

On August 4, 2019, Simone gave birth to a healthy boy and girl. The boy was named Charles Henry Hamilton. Charles, in keeping with Charlie's family tradition, and Henry after Henry Smith, Judy's father. To avoid confusion in the household, they planned to call him Henry. The girl was named Margaret Smith Hamilton. Margaret, after Simone's mother, and Smith after Virginia Smith. They planned to call her Maggie.

Simone spent many hours sitting and staring at the two bundles of loveable and huggable beings. She wanted to hold them forever, and never let go, until complete exhaustion, or a crying baby snapped her back to reality.

Charlie took paternity leave for a month, and did the food shopping and cooking. Anna Maria, their housekeeper, came twice a week to do heavy cleaning, and supplied Simone and Charlie with enough baked ziti, wedding soup, and eggplant parmigiana to feed an army.

"You need your strength, Simone," Anna Maria would say in her broken English. "I make you pastina with egg and cheese."

"Don't fuss," Simone called after her, though she thoroughly enjoyed her cooking.

Anna Maria scurried off to the kitchen, where pots and pans rattled, while she cheerfully hummed with joy doing what she loved the most: cooking for others.

Simone loved being the center of attention, and how she was royally pampered by those around her. But her heart craved the attention and love of Mrs. Smith and Irene. The two had cared for Simone during the darkest days of her young life, and she wanted them now, during these happier times.

Two weeks later, Simone's wish came true. The ladies moved in next door, and the over-abundant cooing and caring of the babies began. Having the babies supervised by the women allowed Simone to go to the office a few days a week. But after a few hours at "I Do", Simone was exhausted. She was happy to return home, and get some much-needed sleep.

Having the duo close by was a blessing to the new parents. And the babies were equally a gift to Mrs. Smith, who was feeling depressed after the sudden death of her husband, Henry. She now had something to look forward to, something to do, and others to love. She spent many days in Virginia, sitting in the porch rocker, searching for renewed meaning to life since Henry's death.

Irene was more of a family member than paid staff. She shopped and cooked for Mrs. Smith and herself, and sat at the same table with her employer, instead of being in the kitchen. This never happened while Mr. Smith was alive. "I know my place," Irene would say whenever she was invited to join the family for meals. But now, as a widow, Mrs. Smith welcomed the company of her long-time confidant and friend. The southern traditions of having a housekeeper out of sight were long gone, and the two women welcomed the change.

Their relationship spanned over forty years, and had developed into a deep and loyal bond. No matter what happened in each other's lives, they were there for each other.

$\mathcal{S}ix$

September 2019

Jennifer phoned Simone at eleven o'clock, waking her from a nap.

"Hello?" she answered in a groggy voice.

"Oh, I thought you'd be up by now," Jennifer apologized.

"I just got the babies down for a nap. I thought I'd catch up on sleep, too. Mrs. Smith and Irene went grocery shopping." Simone looked over at the clock radio for the time. "Oh my, I've been sleeping longer than I thought. I put the babies down at nine o'clock. Okay, I'm awake now. What's up?" she asked with a lilt in her voice.

"We've got an interesting client," Jennifer said. "I need to run the situation past you before we agree to meet with the woman and her mother. They're coming in at two o'clock tomorrow, and I'm stumped as to how to handle this. The bride is requesting us to plan a sologamy ceremony."

"Really!" Simone said, enthusiastically, bolting up from the bed. "I've read about these ceremonies, but never thought we'd be asked to plan one. This is exciting, Jennifer."

"What the hell is it?" asked Jennifer. "I mean, do people *really* marry themselves?"

"Yes," Simone said, "people do marry themselves. As you know, in modern times, there are all sorts of ceremonies. Obviously, it's not a traditional wedding as we're accustomed to planning."

Holding the phone under her chin, she quickly threw on jeans and a tank top. "Jen, I'm going to check on the babies. I'll call you back after Mrs. Smith and Irene return from errands. Meanwhile, I'll call our former intern, Leslie in New York. I remember she mentioned an associate working on a sologamy ceremony. Can you research the trade blogs?"

"I haven't heard you this excited, Simone, since we booked the job in Paris."

"Well let's hope this one doesn't have the same results as that wedding. We don't need another bridal party death looming over us. We'll become known as the 'wedding killers," Simone said, jokingly.

"I hope that never happens. Let me know what ideas and insights Leslie has. Until then, kiss-kiss the babies for me."

Simone tiptoed into the nursery and checked on the sleeping twins. She partially closed the door, picked up the baby monitor from her bedroom, went out on her deck, and called Leslie.

Leslie had been an intern at "I Do" for one year. She was young, attractive, a hard worker, and a fast learner. Leslie loved the wedding planning business, and readily took to the workload. She never complained, and she took the insults from the bridezillas and motherzillas in stride. Leslie's pockets always contained a stash of cool breath strips, two mini bottles of water, lip gloss and a hankie to wrap around the bride's bouquet, in case of unexpected tears. Her favorite moment was being the last person to see the bride before she walked down the aisle.

Every bride who worked with Leslie loved her style, her calmness, and her professionalism. Simone offered her a position at "I Do" but Leslie claimed she wanted to work in Manhattan, where the pace was faster, the weddings bigger, and the pay three times what Simone could offer. Most weddings at "I Do" had a starting budget of $250,000. In the firm where Leslie now worked, the starting budget was $5,000,000.

"When you get tired of the fast pace, Leslie, give me a call. There's always a position for you here."

"That might happen sooner than later, Simone. It's becoming impossible to keep up with the rat race. I haven't had a vacation in over two years. Next week I'm flying to Monte Carlo for a wedding. A big shot in the oil industry is spending $45 million on his little girl's wedding to a Prince. The bigger the wedding, the bigger the problems."

"Yes, I know what you mean," Simone said.

Leslie shared her experience as an assistant planner at a sologamist wedding last year. The women talked about the psychological aspects, and how society often puts lots of pressure on women who are older and not married. Then, after the women marry, they are questioned why they don't have children.

"Aren't you happy we live in a free country?" Leslie asked. "Can you imagine someone marrying themselves in a country where citizens don't have these freedoms?"

Simone took copious notes during their conversation. She did some additional research, and came to the conclusion that, for some women, this wouldn't be such a bad idea. Simone questioned what would happen if a woman met a man in the future who wanted to get married. Would she have to divorce herself? She hoped this wouldn't be brought up at tomorrow's meeting, but it did give Simone a few thoughts to ponder.

$\mathcal{S}even$

1920s – 1950s

Antonio and Betty Taormina were sharecroppers in Mascali, Sicily, where they worked in the fields twelve to fourteen hours a day. Their one-room stone house had dirt floors, and didn't have running water or electricity. In exchange for half of their harvests, the landlord gave Antonio lodging, and a small amount of funds. Life was physically hard, with little possibility of a better future. Local political upheavals and violence became commonplace.

After the last harvest in 1925, Antonio wrote to his cousin, Frank, in America, asking for help. He yearned for a better life for his wife and newborn, Evelyn. Over the next three years, letters were passed between cousins, money was sent, and eventually, documents for passage were purchased. In the middle of the night on November 1, 1928, Antonio, Betty and their young child fled the town of Mascali, and started their journey to America. They walked for miles, hitched rides, and eventually arrived at a port. They traveled across the Atlantic in steerage for nine days. Finally, they arrived at Ellis Island on November twenty-second.

Their cousin, Frank, waited as they went through Customs, finally exchanging hugs, tears and kisses. Antonio and Frank had met only once before, in 1920, when his family left Sicily and headed to America. Frank's family had begged Antonio's parents to join them, but they had refused, fearing the unknown.

"Antonio, you left just in time. Did you hear that Mascali was destroyed by Mt. Etna on November fourth?"

Antonio and Betty made the sign of the cross, remembering their family and friends, who were most likely killed in the eruption. "God have mercy on their souls," Betty whispered.

Frank took them to his modest home in Mt. Vernon, New York, where his wife, Rosalie, had prepared a feast for their arrival. They had never seen such opulence, wealth or abundance of food.

"This is too much," Antonio said.

"Nonsense. Today is a special occasion," Rosalie said. "We don't eat like this every day; just on special days, like today."

Quite often, Antonio had to remind himself he was in another country. Frank and Rosalie made them feel at home, as if they had always belonged. Their baby, Evelyn, thrived from the all the love and attention.

"I can never repay you, Frank, for all you've done for my family," Antonio told his cousin.

Frank, a man of few words, simply said, "What is family for?"

They all lived together for three years. Antonio and Betty spent their days learning English, and adjusting to their new life. Although it was difficult melding into the community, they persevered. Antonio worked six days a week as a contractor for his cousin's electrical company. Over the next decade, he graduated to apprentice, and eventually, a licensed electrician. Betty took in sewing, and earned pin money, from which she contributed a portion towards household expenses.

Their hard work paid off. They saved enough to put a down payment on a house next door to Antonio's cousin. It was an old Victorian that needed a great deal of renovations. They continued to live with their relatives until the house was repaired and brought up to livable conditions. It took six months before they could move, and it took several more years to get the house to a fully restored state. Betty and Antonio didn't care if they lived with creaking wooden floors or peeling wallpaper. They came from a house with a dirt floor and cold, stone walls. To them, they were living the American dream.

Three years after moving into their home, Betty gave birth to a second girl, Adele. Evelyn, now six, treated the baby as a living doll, feeding her a bottle and changing her diapers.

By the time Evelyn was twelve, she had grown tall and thin, like her mother, and Adele grew to be short and stocky, like her father.

The girls' relationship began to change when Evelyn reached high school, and started noticing boys. Babysitting then became more of a chore. She preferred talking on the phone with her friends. When Evelyn was a senior in high school, she began dating a classmate, Sean Wight. His family were immigrants too, from Ireland. His skin was fair, he had bright blue eyes, and jet-black hair.

After graduating from high school, Sean attended Fordham University, and Evelyn took a job as a secretary at the Sanborn Map Company in Pelham, a few miles from home. The couple continued to date, often at the objection of her parents.

Evelyn's parents weren't happy their daughter was seeing a man who wasn't Italian. Although Sean was a bright and ambitious young man, Betty preferred Evelyn be with someone who understood their customs.

"He's not one of us," she implored. "Seek the love of an Italian man."

"But mama, I love him, and he loves me."

"You should date other men," Antonio would chime in.

"Who? I work at a map company where there are old, married men. I don't want to go to nightclubs and bars to find a husband."

Betty realized the more she pushed Evelyn to date others, the more she was actually pushing her towards Sean. She backed off, assuming her daughter would come to her senses. She had to accept that she loved this man, and there wasn't anything she could say or do to change her daughter's feelings.

One evening, Evelyn shared her parents' objections with Sean. He confessed that his parents felt the same way; they'd wish he'd date an Irish lassie, preferably someone from the 'old country.'

But he wouldn't go along with their provincial thinking.

"Marry me, Evelyn," Sean proposed one night. "I can't imagine my life without you."

"I feel the same way," she said. "I love you, Sean, and I want to spend the rest of my life with you." Evelyn truly believed she would wither away and die without him. "But let's wait just a little while," she said. "Maybe in two years after you graduate from Fordham. Meanwhile, I'll continue to save money towards our future."

However, their dream of being together fast-forwarded to the next month when Evelyn announced to Sean that she was pregnant. Two days later, they eloped to Elkton, Maryland, where there wasn't a waiting period for a marriage license.

Shortly after the ceremony, Evelyn called her sister. "Adele, Sean and I just got married."

"Oh my God, Evelyn! You know papa is going to kill you. What do I say if they ask me where you are?" she added.

"Don't tell them. We want it to be a surprise."

Adele ran to her bedroom, locked the door, and wrote in her diary. At fourteen, all she could do was fantasize what it would be like to be with a man. Her sister was so lucky. Adele stayed in her room until she heard Sean's car pull up to the house. She opened her bedroom door, but she didn't venture any further. She simply listened. She expected to hear yelling and screaming. Instead, Adele heard her sister speaking in a calm, even tone.

Evelyn said, "Mama, you and papa were young, and you followed your dreams when you left Sicily. Sean and I want to start a new life together, and follow our dreams, too."

Betty grabbed a kitchen chair and sat down. She was shocked by the news, but also felt a deep sadness that she would never see her eldest walk down the aisle as a bride. She looked at the young couple, and realized what she wanted for her daughter's life wasn't the same. She faced a crossroad: throw her daughter out, or accept her decision to marry. Instead, Betty rose and hugged her daughter. Going against her true feelings, she hugged Sean, as well. Antonio shook hands with his new son-in-law, and grudgingly welcomed him into the family.

"Do your parents know?" Betty asked him.

"No, not yet. We wanted to tell you first," he said.

"And where will you live?" Betty asked.

The question was answered by the stunned expression on the couple's faces. They hadn't thought about that. They were only focused on getting married, and keeping her secret safe.

"You are welcome to stay here," Betty said.

"Oh, Mama," Evelyn cried. "You're being so understanding."

Her father, feeling somewhat defeated as if they had no other choice, finally succumbed and chimed in, "I'll get contractors here to finish the attic. We'll build a small apartment for you." But unbeknownst to them, that promise would take two years to be completed, with much expense, both financially, and emotionally.

Eight

Evelyn had planned to wait a few weeks before she told her parents about her pregnancy. The couple snuggled in Evelyn's twin bed, which they found quite enjoyable. Each night, Adele pressed her ear against the common wall to her sister's bedroom, hoping she'd hear them having sex, or listening in on their private conversations. One night Adele heard more than she had bargained for:

"When are we going to tell your parents about the baby?" Adele heard Sean say.

Baby! Adele almost shrieked the word. *My sister is having a baby!*

"Not yet," Evelyn said. "I'd like to wait a while before saying anything."

"But won't they get suspicious when you start to show, and they figure out you were pregnant before the wedding?"

Oh my God, she had sex before she was married, Adele realized. *No wonder they eloped.* She had so much fodder for her diary, she'd be writing for days.

"We can always say it was a honeymoon baby. Let's not worry about that now, honey. Let's just enjoy being together."

Soon Adele got what she had hoped for – serious moaning coming from her sister on the other side of the wall.

When the couple told her parents, the news was received with great joy and excitement. "It must have happened on our wedding night," Evelyn said, blushing slightly. "The doctor thinks I'm four months along."

Her mother had suspected her daughter's pregnancy, as she had observed Evelyn's tight-fitting clothes had revealed a slightly swollen belly. Her daughter was a married woman, and it wasn't her place to ask questions. Her own mother had been respectful of her life, and of the decisions she and Antonio had made. She wanted to pass on the same reverence to her daughter. It wasn't about why they hadn't said anything sooner. If Evelyn wanted her parents to know, she would have told them.

"Oh, to have the sound of a baby in the house again," her mother said.

Evelyn looked at her mother, who seemed to have aged before her eyes. She hadn't noticed earlier the sallow look on her face. Or, how thin she had gotten. Was she ill, she wondered? Certainly, she would have said something. Evelyn's eyes moved to her father's face, and saw a deep sadness in his eyes, now shadowed with dark circles. When had they grown so old, she wondered? Her parents were obviously pleased they were going to be grandparents, but she felt they were hiding something from her.

Finally, the big day arrived. Evelyn gave birth to a baby girl they named Wanda, meaning "wanderer" like her parents and grandparents. The child had downy soft blond curls and big blue eyes. Adele's joy was palpable. She had a real baby to play with, unlike the plastic dolls she had as a child.

Wanda slept in a bassinet in Evelyn and Sean's bedroom. Over the next year, the small room became too crowded for the three of them. The baby's cries woke up the entire household. It was agreed that Evelyn, Sean and Wanda would move down the hall to her parent's large master bedroom with its own bathroom. Betty and Antonio moved their bedroom to a small maid's room, with a bathroom on the main level, which was most welcomed as they were finding it more difficult to climb the stairs.

Antonio promised to start work on the attic, restoring it into a full apartment for Evelyn's family. It took several months working with an architect, an engineer, and obtaining town permits. Schedules were coordinated, while the town placed one code violation after another in the way of completing the work. It was a never-ending battle for Antonio. One morning, while facing another setback, he said to his wife, "I think it would have been cheaper to buy Evelyn her own home."

Finally, the electrical, HVAC and plumbing were completed. The only work remaining was installing walls and floors, and painting the entire apartment. Soon, the couple would have their own place, and much needed privacy.

Nine

1990 – 2018

Marcelo Pérez worked for his brother's construction company as a day laborer. A native of Cuba, he and his family had escaped from the Communist ruler, Castro. His parents lived in Miami, but Marcelo fled the state after he was arrested for stealing a car. He did the minimum jail time, and then took off. His cousin in New Rochelle suggested he come north to work during the summer, and get away from the temptations and heat of Florida.

Marcelo was a strapping man in his early thirties. He often worked bare-chested, showing off his muscular, toned body. The first time Adele snuck up to the attic to check him out, he was shirtless and sweat covered his chest. She thought he was the sexiest man she had ever seen. Her libido suddenly sprang to life.

One brutally hot August day, the heat unbearably stifling, Adele brought Marcelo two bottles of cold Coca-Cola. She paused for a few moments before making herself known, observing his well-built body as he carried a large piece of sheetrock across the room. Beads of sweat slowly streamed down from his hairy well-formed chest, and past his worn leather tool belt.

"Hi," she said, shyly announcing her arrival. "I brought you something to drink."

They locked eyes. A smile crossed his rugged, dirt-smeared face when he saw the bottles of Coke.

He lifted one to his mouth, while Adele drank in his body. *He's gorgeous,* she thought.

He caught her staring at him, and so she immediately averted her eyes away from his chest and up to his face. He was amused by her embarrassment and flushed face. Slowly, he unabashedly surveyed her equally enticing and full-figured body. Adele wasn't thin, like her sister. She was a fully-formed woman with ample breasts and wide hips, looking more like a twenty-year old rather than a girl of sixteen. Marcelo liked what he saw, and Adele liked that he noticed her.

He leaned in and kissed her on the cheek. "Thank you for thinking of me," he whispered, lingering longer than necessary.

"You're welcome," she barely muttered. Her eyes remained closed. Her heart pounded in her chest. The smell of his body, a mixture of musk and perspiration filled her nostrils.

For the next three days, Adele visited Marcelo, delivering ice cold drinks and snacks. And for three days, he toyed with her emotions. He knew he was arousing her sexual desires, and he enjoyed every moment of this cat-and-mouse game.

"Please stay," he said one day. "Sit and talk while I finish. I like your company."

As he worked, he asked her about her friends, her favorite subjects in school, and if she had a boyfriend.

"Oh no, my parents won't let me date," she announced. She decided she sounded like a foolish child.

"How old are you?" he asked.

"Sixteen."

"A beautiful woman like you would break some hearts," he said smiling at her. "I'm going to miss you," he added.

"What do you mean?" she said with panic in her voice.

"Today is my last day here. Your father will finish the rest."

"No, that can't be," she said sounding desperate. "You can't leave." She knew she was behaving like a silly schoolgirl with a crush, but at that moment, she couldn't imagine days without him, and the routine they had established.

Marcelo saw an opportunity in this young girl with an obvious yearning. He knew exactly what he wanted, and how he was going to get it. He walked up to Adele and stopped inches from her. He stared into her eyes for several moments, and smiled. Her breathing increased. He enjoyed seeing her body's reaction to his presence. He leaned in and kissed her gently. She gave out a timid moan in response. He kissed her again, this time with deep passion and longing until she finally surrendered.

Things happened quickly: Marcelo removed her tank top and unsnapped her bra. Finding no resistance, he gently lowered her pants.

"Do you want to do this?" he whispered as he kissed her breasts.

"Yes . . . yes . . . absolutely," she moaned.

"You're sure?"

"Yes," she repeated, hardly able to breathe.

There, on the newly installed hardwood floor, they made love. She had never been with a man, and the sensations were not what she had expected. It was painful, and suddenly an overwhelming sense of shame and guilt washed over her. *What had she done? What if her parents came into the room?* Her thoughts were interrupted by Marcelo's impulsive whisperings.

"Run away with me to Miami," he announced, unexpectedly.

"Miami?" Adele asked, confused. "Why Miami?"

"That's where I live. I'm going back tomorrow to my family."

"Your family? Do you mean your parents?"

"Not exactly," he said avoiding her question.

"Are you married? Do you have a wife?" The words stuck in her throat, fearing the answer.

"Don't you worry, mi pequena. I will take care of you, set you up in an apartment. It'll be fun."

Adele bolted up, grabbed her clothes and began dressing, suddenly feeling embarrassed for Marcelo having seen her naked.

"What's wrong? Didn't you enjoy our lovemaking?"

She was lost for words. How could she be so stupid as to let a man much older than she trick her into having sex? She no longer felt sixteen; she felt old and foolish.

"I'm fine," she muttered. 'I think I hear my father." With that, she bolted from the attic and ran to her room. She never saw Marcelo again.

Adele didn't tell anyone, other than her diary, what had happened between her and Marcelo. All the love stories she had read in her teen magazines were lies. Love wasn't kisses and butterflies. Love was nothing more than heartbreaks, broken promises and pain. She vowed never to have sex again for as long as she lived.

This was a promise she kept until her final days.

As the weeks passed, Adele's heartbreak over Marcelo's departure increased. *Time will heal your broken heart* she had read in a teen magazine. But that didn't seem to be true. Her sadness ravaged her body to the point that she threw up most mornings. She often felt light-headed and dizzy. She couldn't control her emotions. She found it hard to focus on her schoolwork. *What's wrong with me,* she wondered.

She found comfort in food, especially salty, fatty foods and chocolate. Her mother began noticing Adele's increased appetite and weight gain.

"Are you okay, Adele?" her mother asked one day. "You seem sad. We can't help but notice that you've put on weight. Are you feeling well?"

"Mama, there's something wrong with me. All I think about is food. I'm hungry all the time. And, I'm getting fat."

"Maybe you're going through a growing spurt," her mother assured her. "Is everything okay at school?" She hesitated a moment before asking, "Is there a special boy you like at school?"

Adele burst into tears. As Betty held her in her arms, she listened, with horror, to Adele's story about her puppy love for Marcelo. Her mother's recent questions about Adele's weight gain, and increased appetite suddenly became clear.

"Did he touch you, Adele?"

Fresh tears flowed. Her head, now resting on her mother's chest, nodded up and down. "I haven't gotten my period for three months."

"Did he *rape* you?" The word, rape, stuck in her throat, but she had to ask.

"No. I love him, Mama. But now he's gone."

"We'll go see the doctor as soon as possible," she said firmly. "Meanwhile, don't worry about a thing."

The doctor confirmed their suspicions: Adele was pregnant. She was fifteen weeks along, and the baby was expected in May.

The doctor spent a long time assuring mother and daughter that the baby was fine. But they needed to make some decisions, and fairly quickly. The questions flew past Adele's ears. Her mind was racing, as she was overcome with the reality of the situation.

"Adele will have to leave school," the doctor was saying.

"Obviously," her mother agreed. "The nuns at St. Patrick's wouldn't allow an unwed mother to be in school."

Adele felt suddenly nauseous, dizzy, and about to faint.

"Do you want to keep the baby?" the doctor kept asking her.

She heard her mother's comforting voice. "We have a relative in Rochester, New York that might be able to help. We'll say that Adele is going to travel to Sicily to visit family for a year. Since we are approaching the Christmas break, it will be a good time for her to leave school. No one needs to know," Betty assured Adele and the doctor.

When they got home, Adele went directly to her room, while her mother made phone calls, and decisions.

When she told Antonio about his daughter's pregnancy, he yelled, "That son-of-a bitch. I'll kill him. He comes into my home and assaults my baby."

"Antonio," Betty whispered. "Please, Adele is upset, and yelling isn't going to make things better."

Her husband put his head in his hands, rubbing his face with his calloused, rough fingers. "What are we going to do? What are our relatives and the neighbors going to say? We'll have to leave our church," his words trailed off thinking about the embarrassment Adele had brought to his family.

"I've been thinking, Antonio. I've come up with a plan, if Adele agrees." She discussed her idea with her husband, hoping he would agree, too.

That evening they took Evelyn and Sean out for dinner, leaving the sixteen-year-old, Adele, to babysit her niece, Wanda.

"We have a family situation," Betty said while she buttered a chunk of freshly-baked Italian bread. "It's your sister, Adele."

"Is she ill?" asked Evelyn. "We've noticed she seems withdrawn, and constantly has her head in the refrigerator, looking for something to eat."

"She's not ill," Betty said apprehensively. She remained silent for a few minutes, choosing her words carefully.

Running out of patience, Antonio filled the empty air. "She's pregnant," he screamed. "The bastard contractor who worked on the attic knocked her up."

"Shh," Betty snapped. "You want everyone in the restaurant to know our business?"

Evelyn was speechless. "I can't believe it. She's such a bookworm, always by herself . . . this is the last thing I'd expect would happen. What is she going to do? Is she getting an abortion?" she asked.

Her mother's mouth dropped open. "Evelyn, don't talk like that. You know that's a sin."

"Well, it's legal now. If she's not too far along . . ."

Betty, who was considered the calm, even-tempered

woman in the family, was adamant. "I said, *do not* bring up that subject again."

"Okay, okay," Evelyn said, backing down.

"Your father and I have been discussing sending Adele to a home for unwed mothers in Rochester, New York. They can care for her until she gives birth. She'll have some time to think about putting the baby up for adoption."

"We'll take it," Sean said, without considering Evelyn's opinion.

Three sets of adults' eyes locked onto him.

"Sean," Evelyn said to her husband. "Don't you think we should discuss this before saying we'll take a child?"

"What's there to discuss?" Sean asked. "We've talked about having a second child. A playmate for Wanda would be wonderful. We'll raise them as siblings."

"I have a confession to make," said Betty, interrupting the uncomfortable moment between her daughter and son-in-law. "I was actually going to ask if you would consider adopting Adele's baby. We will help you with expenses."

"What does Adele think about this?" Evelyn asked.

"We haven't told her of our plan. We wanted to discuss it with you two first, and then tell Adele what the four of us have agreed. She's still a child, and can't make such a life-altering decision by herself."

"What about school?" Evelyn asked.

"The nuns at the home will have regular classes for her.

She'll graduate high school around the time of the birth. Part of the admissions program policy is to have the girls stay during the summer and help the nuns with farming, cleaning, and being mentors to the other pregnant girls. Staying busy will help keep their minds off their troubles. Come late August, Adele will go away to college for four years."

"Will she ever come home again?" Sean asked.

"Of course. She'll always have a home with us, but it will be best for her to focus on her studies rather than on the child she's given up. Of course, if you two decide not to adopt the baby, we'll encourage Adele to put it up for adoption through Catholic Charities."

"I don't know," Evelyn said. "It's going to be a very uncomfortable situation when she does come home. And how do we explain this to Wanda? Won't she think it weird that all of a sudden Adele is gone, and then a few months later we have a new baby?"

"Tell her you're expecting a baby. Kids her age don't understand what's going on. Just don't tell her the child is her aunt's."

"She'll find out."

"Not unless you tell her, Evelyn. Right now, our only worry is getting Adele on board with this idea, and being accepted into the home. It will be an ever-developing scenario as time will tell."

"Think about it," Antonio said. "We don't have much time. She's starting to show and we don't want rumors starting at school. Of course, your mother and I will have to tell the nuns at St. Patrick's. Adele won't be the first girl to get pregnant out of wedlock. They'll understand."

They ate their meal in silence, everyone thinking, analyzing, and considering this family dilemma.

The next day, while Adele was in her room studying, Evelyn and Sean spoke to her parents. The couple agreed to take in the baby right after birth. "We'll tell Wanda that I'm going to the hospital. Then, I'll go upstate, and as soon as the baby is discharged, I'll bring him or her home."

"It sounds like a perfect idea," her mother said, resigning herself to the well-thought-out plan. "I think this is the best alternative."

Betty and Antonio shared this news with Adele.

"No, I want to keep the baby," she cried. "No . . . no . . . no. You can't take my baby away from me."

Betty explained her daughter's options, and how it would be best for her to keep the child within the family. Her mother told her that having an infant at seventeen would change her life forever. Her future would revolve solely around the baby, at a time when she should be getting an education, going out with friends and traveling.

Finally, after days of continuous crying jags, Adele agreed to go to Rochester after the Christmas holidays. Through her heartbreak, the abandonment by Marcelo, and the crisis she caused her family, she was grateful. She couldn't live with the thought of never seeing her child again.

During her time at the maternity home, Adele studied home economics, nutrition classes, personal finances, and all the intricacies of running a household. She participated in group therapy, and individual sessions with a psychologist. It was the nuns' hope that through these sessions the girls would be better prepared to separate from their babies, move forward on their own, and become independent women. They'd forgive themselves for their mistake, and make amends with the people they had hurt along the way.

On May 1, 1991, Adele gave birth to a baby girl she named Caroline Olivia. Two days later, her sister, Evelyn, and Sean took Caroline home as their own newborn. Adele cried for days, refusing to eat or socialize with the others. Wanda, of course, was ecstatic to have a baby sister.

Adele stayed at the maternity home for the next three months. During the summer, she focused on harvesting a garden, and helped mentor the arrivals of pregnant girls. It seemed every week another young girl or two were giving up their baby for adoption. Most of them were teenagers, some as young as twelve, while others were older women in their thirties and forties.

Adele heard the screams of the teenagers who had changed their mind after giving birth. In some instances, she saw the cruelty by the nuns who took the child right after birth, and placed the infant into the arms of a young, childless couple.

She was one of the few who got to hold her newborn,

because Caroline was going to be adopted by her sister. The nuns allowed Adele to bond with the baby, albeit for only two days.

At the end of August, Adele went directly from Rochester to the University of Pennsylvania, where she applied and was accepted. She majored in education. She loved to read and study history. Her enjoyment of mentoring the young women convinced her to become a teacher.

She eagerly awaited summers to be free to travel to places she read about only in history books. She couldn't bear to spend these months with her family, where she would see her sister raising Caroline as her own. It was best to spend her time traveling to new lands, away from the reminders at home. The only time Adele got to spend with Caroline was on holidays, birthdays and special occasions. Each time was more painful than the last.

Although the dynamics between the sisters became tense, they still managed to maintain some semblance of closeness. Evelyn was gracious and generous to her sister. She updated her on Caroline's development, and sent her photos regularly. It was difficult for Adele when she saw Evelyn and Sean cuddling, kissing and bonding with her child. But she knew the best life for Caroline was to be raised by her sister. The child had loving parents, and a sister with whom to share her future.

All these years, Adele kept her promise, never telling Caroline that she was her biological mother.

Evelyn tended to her ageing parents' needs. Her

parents left the house only for doctors' appointments or family gatherings. Every two weeks Evelyn took her mother, Betty, to the beauty parlor to have her hair done in the same style she'd sported for sixty years. Her father, Antonio had developed dementia in his late seventies, and died not remembering his wife or family. He had reminisced in lucid detail of his days as a sharecropper in Italy, and had retold the same tales numerous times to anyone who had the patience to listen.

Although Betty's home was filled with her children's, and grandchildren's laughter, she was never the same without Antonio. The two had met when they were children, married young, and by the time they came to America, at the age of twenty, they had experienced many hardships and struggles. Three months after Antonio's death, Betty passed away peacefully in her sleep.

Their will left the house, money and possessions to their two daughters, Evelyn and Adele. It was agreed that since Evelyn never moved from the family home, and was her parent's main caretaker, she would inherit the house. Adele was given cash and several prized possessions, as well as some worthless trinkets, but which had great sentimental value. The two sisters signed a legal agreement, and divided the assets as they each had wished.

Ten

Although Wanda could be sweet, there was also an underlying mean edge about her. She resented Caroline, who seemed to get extra attention, not only from her parents, but also from Aunt Adele and her grandparents. And, there was something pathetic about Caroline that she hated.

When Wanda was a teenager, her sister tagged along with her to the movies. "Take your sister with you," Evelyn would insist. "She doesn't have any friends." Wanda would argue, but in the end, after her mother gave her extra allowance, Wanda agreed to drag her along.

As soon as the two sisters reached their destination, Wanda would dump Caroline. She'd buy her a big bucket of popcorn, an extra-large soda, and Goobers, then tell her to sit rows away from her.

Wanda would meet with her friends, or with a boyfriend. If she and a boy were kissing, she'd threaten Caroline by saying she'd tell their parents how she had continuously caught her gorging on all the cookies in the cupboard. She knew Caroline snuck down to the kitchen in the middle of the night, and ate sweets. Caroline's sweet tooth, in fact, was insatiable, and Wanda held this over her sister. As the years went on, resentment between the two girls grew deeper.

Adele would visit on Sunday mornings, bringing bakery treats, and often, something special for Caroline. Evelyn turned a blind eye to these indulgences, but Wanda watched, and took note. The more attention Caroline got paid from Aunt Adele, instead of her, the more Wanda hated her sister.

Adele's career blossomed. She worked up the ranks from a middle-school teacher, to assistant principal, to eventually, Superintendent of Schools in Nyack, New York. Although she spent a considerable amount of money on vacations, she was frugal during the year, saving whatever she could toward traveling the world.

She lived in a sprawling home, tucked in the hills of Rockland County. There was a community pool, tennis courts, and a large playground within walking distance.

One summer, Adele suggested that her sister stay there while she traveled. "Evelyn, would you and girls like to spend the month of July at my house? I'm going to be in France for the month, and I'd really like someone to watch over the house, water the plants, and tend to my garden."

"That would be lovely," her sister agreed. "I think Wanda and Caroline would love to get away, instead of hanging around every day."

"You'll be able to use the community pool, and all of the other amenities," Adele added.

Evelyn accepted the offer and moved in for the month of July. Although he hated the summer traffic, Sean came up on weekends. They took advantage of this opportunity for several years while Adele was off seeing the world.

When Wanda was nineteen, and more interested in spending her summers with her friends and not at her aunt's home, she decided one evening to explore her aunt's office. She used boredom as justification. She knew what she was doing was wrong, as her aunt had specifically said that she didn't want anyone poking around in her office. This titillated Wanda even more. Wanda felt entitled to do whatever she wanted. So, while the family slept, she snuck into her aunt's office, locking the door behind her.

She snooped inside bookcases, fantasizing about finding a wall safe, or money stashed inside a book. When she didn't find anything interesting, she sat at her aunt's desk, and opened the top drawer. She found a small key belonging to the locked file cabinet. Looking through old paystubs, tax returns, receipts, she came across a large sealed envelope. Written on the outside, "To be opened upon my death." Her curiosity took control; she had to read what was inside.

She stealthily walked to the kitchen and turned on the tea kettle. She placed the envelope over the steam until the flap unglued. Being equally quiet, she tiptoed back into her aunt's study, locked the door behind her again, and let the contents of the envelope spill out onto the desk. Inside was her aunt's will, a birth certificate and adoption papers. Shockwaves tore through her body as she read . . . Marcelo Pérez . . . biological father . . . Sisters of Perpetual Help . . . on and on she absorbed the words.

Then, Wanda read her aunt's will: Caroline would inherit all of her aunt's estate, her possessions, including the huge house, money, and assets. If Caroline were to die prematurely, all assets would revert to Wanda.

That little bitch, Wanda thought as she read through the will. *No wonder she's always hanging around and clinging onto Aunt Adele. I bet she convinced her to give her everything. I wonder if Caroline knows that Adele is really her mother?*

Wanda did a mental calculation, deciding in her uneducated and naive mind that her Aunt Adele was worth millions, which would all go to her bratty, fat sister. She now had another reason to despise Caroline.

Eleven

Years passed and Caroline Olivia Wight spent many of her childhood days watching classmates running around the playground during recess and participating in after-school sports. She wasn't interested in running, soccer, softball, hopscotch, jump rope, or chasing after boys. She didn't want to do anything that caused her to sweat. She also didn't want to be part of a group. Any time she participated in a team activity, she was the recipient of comments and insults because of her size. At eight, she weighed over one-hundred fifty pounds. By high school, she weighed two hundred thirty-five pounds, more than a hundred pounds overweight.

Although Caroline objected, in fifth grade her mother enrolled her in Girl Scouts. "You'll make new friends, Caroline," her mother had assured.

At the third troop meeting, one of the popular scouts raised her hand, and said, "I know who is going to sell the most cookies this year," as she pointed to Caroline. "She'll probably eat them all."

Giggles were immediately followed by a stern reprimand by the Scout Leader. "Samantha, we do not talk about other Scouts in that manner. Apologize to Caroline."

Samantha said she was sorry, but stuck her tongue out at Caroline as soon as the leader's back was turned. Caroline went home crying, and insisted she would never return to that group of mean girls again. Unfortunately, Samantha was probably right: Caroline would have eaten dozens of boxes of cookies, saying other people had ordered them.

Other children poked fun at her, teased her, called her names and no one was willing to play with her. She couldn't help it, she loved food, especially sweets. The doctor had warned her mother that Caroline was headed for high blood pressure, elevated cholesterol and diabetes if she didn't control her eating. But no matter how much her mother monitored her food intake, and prepared healthy meals, Caroline seemed to gain two to three pounds every month.

She found creative ways to hide candy and bags of snacks in her room, inside shoes, under her mattress, and inside pockets of her coats. Once, she returned home from school and found her mattress standing up, leaning against the wall. Her mother never said a word about the stash she had found. Caroline did a mental inventory of the 3 Musketeers and Twix bars she lost. Fortunately, her supply inside her shoes and coat pockets were still there, but from that day forward, she never kept any candy hidden under her mattress. During dinner her mother said nothing. Caroline expected a confrontation, but the silence was enough proof of her disapproval.

Caroline knew she'd need a new hiding place for her sweets. It was only a matter of time before her mother would search her entire room, including her closet, where most of her stash was hidden. She pulled her nightstand towards her, and taped candy bars down the back. Obstructed by the nightstand was a large piece of painted plywood, affixed to the wall by four Phillips head screws. She had never noticed it before, mostly because it was the same color as the blue walls of her bedroom. At once, she retrieved her nail clipper, and using the file, undid the screws. Behind the board was an abandoned cast iron wall register. At first Caroline thought about hiding candy inside. But when she looked, there was a big empty hole leading to nowhere. It must have been a source of heat at one time in the old Victorian home. The honeycomb brass plate was covered with dust, and it was probably home to spiders and other critters. With the covering gone, she could hear echoed conversations taking place in the kitchen, a floor below her bedroom. The thick plaster wall blocked voices, but through the grate, she could hear almost everything being said. Eavesdropping on conversations between the adults became her new hobby.

When Caroline was fourteen, she began menstruating. The pediatrician suggested the young teen be sent to sleepaway camp for overweight children. He assured her parents that camp would be a good way for Caroline to get some physical activity. He quoted studies proving that girls often lost their baby fat once they started getting their periods.

The girls at camp were heavy like her, and equally clumsy at sports. They didn't make fun of each other's weight, as they were all the same, some even heavier than Caroline, and others were thinner. Now, she wasn't the only fat girl in the group, nor the butt of a joke.

She attempted to enjoy the variety of sports offered, but she hated them all, except swimming and horseback riding. When she rode her favorite horse, Darryl, she felt free, just she and the horse alone. The animal listened to all her fears, complaints and confusion about life. He nodded and neighed at all the right moments, as if agreeing with Caroline's woes.

One day Caroline rode Darryl to the far end of the pasture, where she dismounted and sat under a tree. While the horse grazed nearby, she felt content and happy. There wasn't anyone telling her what to do, what to eat or not eat, or judging her. She loved Darryl, and she knew the horse loved her, too. As she dozed, her thoughts recalled a conversation between her mother and her mother's sister Adele.

"Did you tell her?" Adele whispered.

"No."

"Why haven't you told her? You said you would once she turned thirteen."

"Adele, stop asking. We don't intend to tell her. Ever. So, stop asking. And don't you, either," her mother said in a slightly raised voice.

"Never?"

Then the two went back to whispering. Caroline could only hear a word here or there. Something about their mother - her grandmother - being mean . . . nuns . . . a farm in upstate New York . . . a man named Marcelo. She was curious what it all meant. She couldn't ask her mother, because then she'd have to reveal the discovery of the hidden grate.

Caroline pondered this secret, as she fantasized different scenarios. Maybe they were going to send her to a boarding school, or educate her about sex (which she already knew), or worse: perhaps her parents were getting a divorce. But they would have told her last year. The thought of her parents divorcing frightened her. Who would she and her sister live with? She suddenly wished she had some candy to comfort her. She could almost taste those gooey creamy caramel milk chocolate treats, taped to the back of her nightstand, which she prayed would still be there upon her return from camp.

When it was time for lights out, Caroline heard candy wrappers crumpling. Although sweets were strictly forbidden, parents often tucked special treats into their children's suitcases. This not only circumvented camp rules, but undermined their intentions for sending their overweight child to this camp. Parents who didn't know how to show their love, other than with food, felt this was a sure way their child would know they were loved and missed by those left behind at home. The girls who had the forbidden candy threatened the others if they ratted them out. They never shared their treasures. It was theirs, and theirs alone. The candy was secretly consumed in the dark, while the others felt jealous and abandoned by the parents who didn't love them enough to hide candy in their suitcases, too. Caroline fantasized about the day when camp ended, and she could go to the candy store, buy candy and eat it in the dark. The only secret stash Caroline's parents put in her suitcase was sugar-free chewing gum. Obviously, they didn't love or miss her, she concluded.

Caroline's obligatory letters home were short, saying she missed her parents, and her sister. She didn't, of course, miss her sister, but knew she had to include her name in her correspondence. Unlike Caroline, her sister Wanda was tall, thin, blond and very popular. Caroline imagined Wanda in a bikini at the beach with friends, or a boyfriend, laughing and enjoying herself. *She's probably having a great summer, while I'm stuck with a bunch of other fat kids,* Caroline mused.

Caroline wrote about how the food at camp was bland and awful. Portions were small, and sometimes indistinguishable from meal to meal. Desserts were filled with sugar-free chemicals, and the only sweet drink available was diet soda, which Caroline drank pitchers full. The water was ignored, as the mineral and sulfur taste made her stomach turn. But what Caroline missed most of all, she couldn't describe in her letters, namely listening to the whispered conversations through the old bedroom grate while she gorged on her secret stash of candy and bags of junk food.

She returned home ten pounds lighter, but feeling ten pounds heavier in her heart, and feeling punished for being the way she was. She hated camp, hated her bunkmates, hated being fat. She couldn't help the cravings, the daydreams, and the inability to stop eating whenever food was amply available. Mostly, she missed Darryl the horse.

When Caroline was fifteen, she refused to go to church with her parents and her sister. She never gave them a reason, other than she found Mass boring, and no longer believed in the religious rituals. She and her parents had minor arguments, but after a few Sundays, they acquiesced, and let Caroline sleep in while they went off to church. These two hours of separation gave Caroline the opportunity to eat without fear of her mother walking into her bedroom, and being caught red handed. Once she heard her father's car drive away, she'd jump out of bed, look through the cupboard and refrigerator, and nibble on a cornucopia of different foods: two olives from an opened jar, a scoop of leftovers, a tablespoon of ice cream, a few saltine crackers, or a handful of potato chips from an opened bag. She doled it all out carefully, making sure to appear as though no food was missing.

Aunt Adele arrived every Sunday for brunch. She'd bring a bag of freshly baked assorted bagels, a large container of cream cheese, and sometimes a package of thinly sliced smoked salmon. For dessert, she also bought whatever looked good that day: a strawberry shortcake with an abundance of freshly whipped cream and in-season juicy strawberries, or a flaky crumb cake that left fingers covered with sweet confectioner's sugar, or a silky-smooth coconut custard pie.

Evelyn provided the coffee, and an omelet of thinly-sliced white potatoes, sweet onions, and aromatic fresh dill. Or, she'd cook a hearty sweet sausage and cheese casserole, putting all the ingredients together the night before, so the day-old challah could absorb the rich creamy liquid.

It was Caroline's job to put it in the oven before everyone returned from church.

Adele was a short stocky woman, three years younger than Evelyn, and resembled her father, Antonio. Evelyn had her mother Betty's finer features, and slender figure. The siblings had been close since they were children, and had remained that way through adulthood. Each knew the other was always there at the ready to help in any way.

Sadly, this was not true for Caroline and her sister. They looked like complete opposites. Wanda was tall and slender like her mother. Her blond frosted hair accented her fair delicate features and blue eyes. Caroline was short, with mousy brown hair and brown eyes. She didn't bear any similarities to her sister. "You take after your grandfather," her mother would say when Caroline asked why she didn't look like Wanda. "Everyone is different and special."

If Adele got to the bakery when it opened, she'd get an extra treat just for Caroline: two enormously stuffed, raspberry filled jelly donuts. Because they were so popular, these deep-fried delights sold out within minutes.

While Evelyn busied herself in the kitchen Aunt Adele would suggest Caroline look at her latest knitting project. She'd pat her Vera Bradley paisley knitting bag, a secret code meaning there were two glorious jelly donuts hidden inside. Like two little kids they'd rush into Caroline's bedroom, close the door, and dive into them without anyone else knowing about their sweet secret.

Aunt Adele didn't judge, didn't call Caroline fat, and never mocked her. Instead, her aunt showed her great respect, proving how much she truly loved her. Her parents didn't love her the way Aunt Adele did. And, Caroline loved her aunt more than anyone else in the family.

Upon seeing the treats, Caroline's eyes widened with delight. As she devoured the forbidden food, making sure not to drip any jam onto her clothes, Aunt Adele observed, smiling.

"Remember, don't tell your mother," Adele prompted her niece.

"Oh no, I'll never tell on you, Aunt Adele," Caroline assured her as they exchanged hugs. "I remember the first time you brought me donuts, and how my mom got so mad at you."

Adele reminisced, too. That day she promised herself never to replicate that scene.

"You know Caroline is fat, why did you bring her donuts?" Evelyn had demanded.

"It's just a special treat. I meant no harm," her sister had replied sheepishly. "I love all of you, but I especially want to bring something that would put a smile on Caroline's face."

"Yeah, and fat on her hips!"

Caroline had burst into tears, dropped the donut from her hand, and ran up to her bedroom, not coming out again until that evening.

In her room, Caroline had crouched down on the worn oak floor, rested her tear-stained face on her knees, and had listened to the kitchen conversations that wafted into her bedroom through the abandoned heating vent. As she'd listened, she devoured her secret stash of candy until it was depleted and she felt sick.

"Why did you have to say she was fat – especially in front of her?" Adele had asked her sister.

"Because she is," snapped Evelyn. "You both need to face facts. Caroline is fat, and supplying her with donuts isn't helping her.

"Why do you have to be so mean?"

But there had been no response from Evelyn, who continued to prepare the usual Sunday morning feast.

"I'm starting to regret my decision," Adele had suddenly blurted out.

Evelyn had stopped chopping and put down the chef's knife. She'd known exactly what Adele meant, and it had nothing to do with donuts. Evelyn had straightened her back, pushed her shoulders back and turned to face her sister.

"Well, it's a little late for that, don't you think?" Evelyn had said evenly. She'd lowered her voice to a whisper, "You should have thought of that years ago."

Adele had begun crying. Deep haunting sounds emanated from her body. Evelyn then ran to her sister and held her. "I'm sorry I said that. Don't ever regret your decision. Sean and I have never regretted the one we made years ago."

Caroline focused on their words as they had morphed into whispers. She'd pressed her ear up against the cold metal vent, hoping she could hear exactly what the women were saying, but she could not decipher any of it. But she'd known whatever her mother and aunt were discussing was about her. She had won-dered what decision the two women were talking about. Aunt Adele had never married, and Caroline had heard rumors that she had a boyfriend many years ago who broke her heart. Maybe Aunt Adele had decided not to marry him, and that's what they were discussing.

Although Caroline had trusted her Aunt Adele more than anyone she knew, she never told her about the grate. Caroline had felt at ease talking to her aunt about school, boys, and how she wished she had a boyfriend, but not about the secret hole in the wall.

Adele snapped out of her reverie when Caroline said, "I love you so much, Aunt Adele. My mother is so mean to me. Why can't she be more like you?"

"Caroline, many girls don't get along with their mothers at your age. It's normal."

But Adele knew this wasn't always true. Guilt washed over her. Her niece wasn't an attractive girl, and might never have a boyfriend, or ever marry. There were many attributes that Caroline possessed, which reminded Adele of herself at her age.

She's such a sad child, and the donuts help to cheer her up. Or, do I want to keep Caroline fat so she won't be attractive to men, and not get herself pregnant, like me?

Adele realized her feelings were unrealistic and selfish. She cleared her throat, stood up, and with determination said, "Caroline, I have to stop bringing you treats. I know you love them, but I'm not helping you. I'm adding unnecessary calories to your diet, and I shouldn't be sneaking food to you against your mother's wishes."

Caroline embraced her aunt. "Please don't stop. Bringing me donuts shows how much you care."

"Oh my," Adele quickly said. "No, no, my dear, it's not." She pulled her niece from her clutches, and looked into the girl's watery eyes. "It's my way of seeing joy on your face, but it isn't the right thing to do. I'm sorry, but I can't continue. Please understand, Caroline. I love you very much, more than you realize. But I'm really hurting you."

"You could never hurt me, Aunt Adele. I know that I have to lose weight, but it's so difficult."

"I know, darling. I know. I've struggled with weight my whole life, so I know how your feel." She hugged Caroline again as she whispered, "I love you."

"I love you, too, Aunt Adele," Caroline said as tears stained her aunt's blouse.

"Lunch is ready!" shouted Evelyn from the kitchen, breaking the tender moment.

"We're coming," Adele hollered back. Turning to her niece she added, "Caroline. You're like my own daughter," These words stuck in her throat. "But I'm not really showing you love by supplying you with fattening foods. I still want to come to your room, and continue to have our talks. But I fear your mother suspects I'm bringing you treats."

"How? I never told her."

"She told me she found a white bag in your room and asked if I brought you treats from the bakery. I lied, of course, and said no. So, I think it is best that I no longer bring you these temptations. I hope you understand."

"Yes," Caroline finally acquiesced.

"Let's have lunch now," Adele said, as she opened Caroline's bedroom door, and the two stomped down the stairs toward the kitchen.

Twelve

2019-2021

On a brisk mid-September afternoon, Simone met Mrs. Evelyn Wight and her daughter, Caroline, at the office. It was apparent by her expression and body language that she was unhappy about her daughter's decision to have a sologamist wedding. Shortly after a dead-fish handshake and introductions, Evelyn Wight walked quickly into the conference room and claimed a seat at the table. She was dressed in black slacks that hugged her slender body, and a light blue turtleneck that matched her sad eyes. She placed her pocketbook on the chair next to her, and immediately fished out a packet of tissues. She was prepared for tears.

Following close behind was Caroline Wight. Simone observed she wasn't much taller than she; maybe 5'3". Caroline had a thick body frame, and was at least one hundred pounds overweight, making her waddle when she walked. She wore a black oversized blouse with white ruffles at the neckline underneath a black knit sweater. A flowing floor-length black and white striped skirt, completed the look, which wasn't successfully hiding her swollen ankles. She wore thick eyeglasses set inside black frames. When she smiled, the glasses pressed tightly against her ample cheeks, leaving behind oily smudges on the lenses. Her brown eyes were in direct contrast to her mother's. In fact, Simone didn't note any features that made her think they were related.

Before Simone could start the meeting, Evelyn jumped in and proclaimed, "Did Caroline tell you about her ridiculous idea of getting married to herself? It's blasphemous. It's against the laws of nature! I never heard of such a thing."

Simone looked at the woman's angry face. "Yes, I have heard of such weddings. But, before we continue with this discussion, I'd like my associate to join us."

Simone stood by the door and said, "Jennifer, could you please come in to the conference room?"

Jennifer was accompanied by her therapy dog, Goober.

Goober had the body of a Border Collie, the slobbering of a St. Bernard, and the loyalty of a Labrador. He had an innate ability to sense danger, and the skills to alleviate a stressful situation.

Jennifer walked with a cane in one hand and Goober close at foot. The dog wore a bright yellow "Therapy Dog" tag around his neck, attached to a paisley-colored bandana. She struggled in flats, the adverse result of years of wearing stilettos. Due to previous horrific circumstances of an attempted murder, her broken ankle, sustained along with other battered body parts, had taken months to heal. She used the cane, especially upon standing because she occasionally experienced spasms in her insoles and calves. She thought of the stick as a weapon if she ever encountered another precarious situation. Jennifer joined Simone in the conference room, and introduced herself and Goober to the two women.

"Oh, what a sweet dog," Caroline said. "May I pet him?"

"Actually, no," Jennifer affirmed. "He's working." And working he was. He walked directly to Caroline's mother and put his head on her lap, staring up at the woman with pathetic, understanding eyes. Evelyn Wight was startled by his action, and shifted in her chair.

"He senses your distress, ma'am," Jennifer said, "Goober, come." The dog obeyed and plopped down at Jennifer's feet.

"I don't know what to say," Evelyn responded.

"You don't need to say anything," Jennifer said. "Just tell me what the situation is, and Goober and I will figure out a solution," she chuckled, trying to alleviate the apparent tension in the room.

This seemed to calm the older woman. Her anxiety and seeming hostility were quickly quelled.

"Caroline," Simone explained to Jennifer, "wants a sologamy wedding. But Mrs. Wight isn't happy with her daughter's decision, and they've asked for our help settling the differences of opinion."

"Have you ever heard of such a horrible thing?" Evelyn asked. "It's an embarrassment . . . an outrage . . ."

Goober responded with his typical yawn. Simone smiled.

"These weddings have become popular," Jennifer interjected, cutting off Mrs. Wight.

Turning to her mother, Caroline said, "See. It's not such a crazy idea."

"That is not what I said," Jennifer quickly answered. "No disrespect, Caroline, but it is very unusual, and I can see why your mother isn't happy about the idea."

"I told you they'd agree with me," Evelyn snapped.

"Also, no disrespect to you, Mrs. Wight," Jennifer replied. "While it is not unusual, I can understand being concerned. Let's hear what Caroline is thinking, and how we can help."

"Humph," was all Evelyn could muster up.

Simone asked, "Can you tell us why you want this ceremony, Caroline?"

Quickly turning to her mother, Simone added, "I'm going to ask that you do not make any comments until your daughter is finished."

Goober butt-dragged himself back over to Mrs. Wight and put his head on her lap again. "I hope you don't mind," Jennifer said. "He's sensing your discomfort, and wants you to feel safe."

"I don't mind," Evelyn said, giving Goober a gentle tap on the head. "Sorry, I know I shouldn't pet him, but he's so adorable."

"That's fine for the moment. A pat on the head tells him you're feeling better." Turning to Caroline Jennifer said, "Please, Caroline, tell us your story."

"Well, as you can see, I'm fat," she began.

Jennifer remained nonplussed and let Caroline continue. "I've never had a real boyfriend. I had a prom date once, and sometimes I'd ask a friend to accompany me to a wedding. The one boyfriend I had was nasty. My initials spell out COW, and he used to call me his little heifer."

"You never told me that," her mother interrupted. "Who was this boy?"

"Please, Mrs. Wight, let Caroline tell her story." Simone implored.

Caroline was notably upset. Sensing that, Goober walked slowly over to Caroline, and placed his head gently on her thigh. Caroline paused and smiled. "At least the dog understands me."

Evelyn consoled, "Caroline, I hate to see you so upset. It's just . . . it's just . . ."

"It's just if I weren't so fat," stammered Caroline, "I'd be marrying a real man, like you and daddy want me to."

"That's not true," her mother implored. "Daddy and I only want the best for you. You don't care enough about yourself. Maybe if you lost a few pounds, you'd be having a real wedding."

"See, I told you it's because I'm fat. You don't think any man would marry me. Why can't you understand that

I can't just lose weight as easily as you?"

The bickering continued, while Simone and Jennifer looked on.

"You don't understand me. You and daddy never did."

"I'm not paying for this crazy idea. And your father and I will not come to your wedding."

Voices were raised, and it was obvious this discussion was beginning to escalate.

Goober stood up, his ears pointed upward, his tail between his legs. A deep, guttural growl could be heard, followed by a bark. Jennifer performed a hand command, and the dog sat down, but he remained alert, his body ready to respond at a moment's notice.

Simone looked knowingly at Jennifer, the unspoken words between them, obvious. Jennifer was considered the yin to Simone's yang. They worked in complete harmony, frequently sensing each other's thoughts without verbal acknowledgment.

"Caroline and Mrs. Wight," Simone said, putting one hand on top of Caroline's, and the other on Evelyn's, which halted the accelerating argument. "There seems to be an abundance of emotions rising to the surface," Simone said with a soothing and empathetic tone. "Caroline, I'd like to suggest you discuss your feelings with us privately."

"I can take a hint," Evelyn replied furiously, her feelings obviously hurt.

Simone turned to her and said, "Mrs. Wight, there are times in a girl's life when she can't tell her mother everything. I'm sure you kept things from your own mother when you were a young girl."

Evelyn was about to object, but Simone cut her off. "I'm sure you kept a secret diary or had stolen kisses you never spoke about." Simone knew she had hit a nerve by the flash of recognition in Evelyn's eyes. "How about you sit in our reception room? One of the associates will bring you some refreshments." She assisted her from her chair as though she needed help. Simone opened her office door, and called for Sylvia, one of the office interns.

"Please deliver Mrs. Wight to our reception area, and bring her some refreshments."

"Certainly," Sylvia said, obligingly.

Simone closed the door to the conference room, faced Caroline and said, "Okay, tell us the truth: why do you want to marry yourself? Or, is it just to torture your mother?"

This statement seemed cruel, unlike Simone's usual professional demeanor, but it conveyed a message to the young woman that Simone and Jennifer meant business. "There is obviously some tension between the two of you, and it's apparent you want to marry yourself to make a point."

Simone continued, "Our company has never worked a sologamist wedding but that's not to say we can't, or won't. What I *am* saying is, we don't want to waste your time or ours, or anyone's money on a vendetta."

Simone sat down across from Caroline and continued her questioning, "I'd like to know *why* you

want this ceremony. You've shared that you think because you are fat, no one wants to marry you. I'm sure
sharing those feelings with us was difficult. But I know
there's more."

Caroline sat quietly; her eyes lowered. When she
became more composed, she adjusted herself in the
chair to face her 'firing squad.' The chair squeaked under
her bulk.

"I've been fat my whole life," she began. "I've seen
baby pictures of myself, and I was always the chubbiest kid
in the family. I don't look like my sister or any of my cousins,
or even my parents. The other kids at school picked on me,
calling me 'fatty' or 'lardy.' They never wanted to play with
me, and so I found solace in candy bars. Mr. Goodbar and
the 3 Musketeers became my friends. Now, later in life, my
new friends are Wendy's, McDonald's and Burger King."

She paused again to blow her nose. "My sister
had a big, beautiful wedding. I know my parents spent
a lot of money on the affair, and my mother always
said that there's money for my wedding, too." A long
barrage of wishes ensued: "I want a wedding. I want to
wear a gown with a long train and have my daddy walking me down the aisle. I want a big reception with music,
dancing, and a four-tier cake. I want to get married and
have a child. I want a destination wedding. I want what's
coming to me."

"I'm hearing a lot of 'I wants," Simone said.

"Don't you think I deserve a wedding, or be married?"

"Tell me about your sister," Simone said.

"Why do you want to know about *her?*" asked Caroline with a contemptuous tone.

"Because you seem to want what she has."

Caroline remained silent before answering.

"Yes, I do want what she has: a loving husband, a beautiful little girl, and a big house. My sister is happy. I want to be happy, too."

"Is she thin?" Jennifer asked.

Caroline looked startled, and hesitated for a moment. "Yes."

"Besides being thin, what else did she do to you to make you hate her?"

"Well, she never wanted me around. I felt as if she was embarrassed to be seen with me because I was bigger than her. My mother had to beg her . . . probably gave her extra money . . . to take me along to the movies, or to school dances. She'd drop me like a hot potato as soon as we got to our destination. And then I had to swear not to tattle that I sat by myself in the movies, or alone in the bathroom until the dance was over."

Caroline blew her nose again. "I've never admitted this to anyone else," Caroline said, her voice cracking. "I'm a closet eater. Figuratively and literally."

Jennifer asked, "What does that mean?"

"I hide candy inside my snow boots, inside my closet, my dresser, and in the car's glove compartment and arm rest."

"Does your mother know about this?"

"I don't think so."

Simone wondered if Caroline now regretted this admission, but she pressed on. "Can you elaborate more?"

Caroline cleared her throat and readjusted herself in the chair. "I go to McDonald's and order food for two, changing up the menu so the mystery woman behind the speaker thinks I'm ordering for another person in my car. I'd get two orders of Quarter-Pounders, one with cheese, one without, and two orders of fries, one with salt and one without. I'd park my car in the restaurant's lot and eat the two orders of food. Afterwards, I'd go home to a cooked meal."

Caroline began crying, shaking her head, embarrassed. "I shouldn't have told you. You must think I'm a freak."

Goober whined and looked up at Jennifer, sensing tension. If she gave him permission, he'd trot over to Caroline and sit by her. "Stay" she said with a hand motion. He laid down near her feet and looked soulfully at her.

"Caroline," Simone said, sympathetically, "you're safe here. What you tell us won't leave this room."

Caroline seemed relieved. She continued. "My mother tries to help. She makes sensible meals for me: a piece of bland fish, a salad, and a green vegetable. But she and daddy get steak, hamburgers, or lamb chops, and potatoes, with lots of butter, or fried chicken or some other fatty foods. She weighs and measures my food, and expects me to eat tiny morsels while they eat substantially larger portions. 'Why should they suffer because you're fat?' my mother would say. Then, afterwards, she complains about the extra work."

Caroline reached into her purse and pulled out a clean tissue, and dabbed at her eyes. "My mother looks at me with disgust. It's obvious I'm not allowed to eat more than what's on my plate, so I substitute my meals by eating before I arrive home. They eat dessert, and she tells me I can't have any. Do you have any idea how that makes me feel? So, after dinner I'd go to my room and sneak candy from my secret stash."

"I see," Simone said. "Are you still eating extra meals before going home?"

"Yes," she whispered.

Jennifer motioned to Goober. He slowly moved to Caroline's side, resting his head on her ample lap, looking up at her sympathetically, with his large droopy eyes.

"I have a dog, too," Caroline said. "For my twenty-fifth birthday three years ago, my parents gave me a toy poodle. My parents thought having a dog to walk several times a day would force me to exercise. I was in charge of getting him housebroken, and to feed him tiny meals. I felt it was their way of telling me if I could control the dog's food portions, I could control my food portions, too."

"What's his name?" Jennifer asked.

"I named him Pyewacket, from the movie, *Bell, Book and Candle*. Of course, my sister teased me about naming the dog after a food. I tried telling her the name is spelled p-y-e, and not p-i-e, but it was just another opportunity for her to taunt me."

Caroline petted Goober's head.

"Did you ask your parents for a dog?" asked Jennifer.

"When I was ten, I asked them for a dog for Christmas. But they said it wouldn't play with me because I was too fat to run. My sister said I'd have to hang a pork chop around my neck so the dog would play with me. She was so mean to me. I bet they thought I'd eat the dog's food, too."

"That's a rather disturbing accusation," Jennifer interjected. "Did your mother say that, or you assumed that?"

Caroline paused, reflecting. "I assumed. But I don't think it's too far from the truth. I actually ate the cat's food once because I was so hungry." She smiled at Goober. "I wish I had a dog like Goober. He seems to understand me, just like the horse I rode at camp."

"He does have the ability to sense when something is wrong, or when someone is upset," Jennifer said.

Caroline was now in a vulnerable state. The more Simone got her to relax and talk about herself, the more she would open up about wanting to marry herself. Now that her mother wasn't present, she continued to speak about their relationship.

"So, you think because of your weight no one can love you, and you'll never find a husband?" Simone asked, trying to get back on the subject. "But yet, the more you eat, the more weight you gain, causing you to fail at being thinner. It's a self-defeating cycle."

"Look at me," stammered Caroline. "I'm twenty-eight years old. I've never been intimate with a man, and I probably never will. The closest I'll get to a lay is with a potato chip," she joked.

Simone wondered how long Caroline had been using that line, but she wasn't going to feed into her self-deprecation.

"Caroline," Simone continued, "You've heard of professional coaches, I'm sure. Such as business, fitness, life and religious coaches."

Caroline nodded.

"I'm a wedding coach. I help couples plan a marriage as well as a wedding. I'm sensing you need a life coach to help you with your goals and direction, and possibly talking to a therapist before you plan your wedding."

"Are you calling me crazy for wanting to marry myself?" Caroline said, scowling.

Simone remained calm, but she had suspected this would be Caroline's reaction. "No, not at all; it's not what I implied. I'm going to ask you again: why do you want to marry yourself?"

"Because I want what's coming to me. I want a wedding."

Simone continued, "You realize that during a wedding ceremony you vow in front of friends and family that you will love and cherish yourself, in sickness and in health. Do you think your lifestyle will warrant you being in good health? Are you showing yourself how much you love yourself by the amount of food you eat? Is food the love you crave? Or, is it simply because you feel you're being cheated since your parents paid for your sister's wedding?"

"Honestly, Caroline," added Jennifer, "food is your enemy, and it's your lover. It's also trying to kill you."

"Food," said Caroline, "is my favorite 4-letter F-word."

Simone and Jennifer couldn't help but chuckle.

"These days," Simone continued, "there are a variety of marriages...same sex marriages, civil ceremonies, commitment ceremonies, and surprise weddings, to name a few. If you don't take care of yourself now or eliminate the closet eating and hiding food, what makes you think that after this ceremony, you'll suddenly change and start taking care of yourself, and love yourself? Finally, how do you see your life evolving after the ceremony?"

"After I get married," Caroline said, "I want to have a baby. Artificial insemination, of course."

"Have you discussed these plans with your doctor? Or with your parents?" Simone asked. "How do you plan to take care of the baby? Will you work, or will your mother help raise the child?

"I guess I never thought of these things. I was so focused on getting married that I didn't think about the future." She gazed off in the distance, envisioning her life as a married woman with a child.

Her response seemed very immature, but not surprising. Simone and Jennifer discovered many couples were so focused on the wedding, but didn't think about what followed. Caroline was focused on the ceremony, and didn't think what would happen to her, or the family dynamics afterwards.

"How did you find our company, Caroline?" Simone asked, snapping the woman back to the present. "What made you call us, and not a wedding planner closer to where you live in Mt. Vernon, New York?"

"I called several planners," Caroline admitted, "but none were willing to work with me. I found you on the Internet, and when I called, I was invited to come and discuss my plans. No one else offered to talk to me before."

"I'm still not convinced, Caroline, that your wedding is a good fit for our company," Simone said. "I do think you need to talk to a professional about your eating habits before you move ahead. If you want to have a wedding, we will certainly work with you. We have no right to judge your decision. I just wanted to point out the obvious issues, no matter how painful they may be."

"Thank you," Caroline said meekly. "You two are the only ones who have listened to me, or suggested I take a closer look at my eating habits, and what will happen to me after the wedding. I know that sounds strange . . . but it's true. Everyone else just told me to stop eating."

Goober stretched, and Caroline smiled at him. "How

come he's a therapy dog?" she asked, turning to Jennifer. "Unless that's too personal a question."

"Not too personal at all," Jennifer said. "I had an accident last year, and Goober helped me get through some dramatic changes in my life. He's my supporter, my protector, and he's a great man-magnet," she chuckled.

"Caroline," Jennifer said seriously, "I had a traumatic experience involving my fiancé. He left me for dead on Charles Island, located a few towns over from here. Afterwards I felt unloved, abandoned and rejected." Caroline's eyes widened. So, she thought, she wasn't the only one who had similar feelings of rejection.

"I was hurt, both physically and emotionally," Jennifer continued. "But with the help of others . . . many others . . . I'm healing. Caroline, please listen to what Simone is recommending. Get some professional help. I had to discover why I was attracted to such a monster, and other bad boys before him. There were red flags, but I ignored them all, because I wanted to get married and have a child. My focus and end goals weren't smart ones. Now, when I think about getting involved with a man, it's for different reasons. Maybe one day I'll get married and have a child, but latching on to just anyone isn't a smart way of going about it."

This startled Simone. She had never heard Jennifer admit to these emotions.

"I got psychological and physical help, Caroline. And I'm much better for it," Jennifer confessed.

Caroline nodded. "Thank you for sharing, Jennifer. I

promise, I'll give your suggestions some thought."

"What do you do for a living?" Jennifer asked.

"I'm an influencer, and I also record audio books. They're two jobs where people don't have to see how fat I am."

"What product do you promote?" Simone inquired.

"Beauty products. A little ironic, in a way. People never see my face or body, but they read my blogs and follow me on social media. I test nail and hair products, and makeup. I do very well," she added.

Simone wasn't convinced Caroline would go through with the ceremony. It was odd, after all, and the reasoning behind her wanting a wedding, was not solid, or well-thought-out. Simone would help Caroline if she wanted a wedding, but she was doubtful, and felt there was less than a twenty percent chance it would actually take place. She believed if she could help Caroline face her food issues, she had done a good deed.

Simone was an astute business woman, and often saw opportunities when others turned a blind eye. She felt planning a sologamist wedding would give her a lot of publicity . . . publicity she could not afford to pass up. If Jennifer agreed, they'd plan Caroline's wedding at a reduced rate. But before they agreed to such an event, Caroline had to do some serious soul-searching and work on herself. No doubt she faced a long road ahead, addressing her inner demons, and the relationship with individual members of her family.

"Do you know where you want this ceremony?" Simone asked, breaking the tension.

"Florida," Caroline answered. "Either on Sanibel Island or Key Biscayne. Many of my relatives have retired and moved to Florida, or they go there for the winter, so it'll be easy for them to attend the wedding."

"Your mother doesn't seem to support this idea," Simone said. "Do you think she'll hinder the attendance?"

"Probably."

"It's obvious she's not happy about your decision to marry yourself. What about your father – does he support your decision?"

"My daddy is always working. He doesn't get involved in such decisions. He's rarely home, and my relationship with him was, and still is, lukewarm. When I was younger, he'd bring me candy. Maybe because he felt guilty for not being around. Whenever I had a problem, he'd tell me to talk to my mother, but that didn't always work out too well."

"I think we've kept your mother at bay long enough," Simone said, as she checked her watch, realizing she needed to get home to the twins. "Contact us once you have an idea of a venue location, and after you've done more serious thinking about how you want to proceed." Simone scribbled a name and number on a piece of paper and handed it to Caroline. "Meanwhile, if you decide you'd like to talk to a therapist, this is whom I'd recommend."

Caroline placed the note inside her bag. Struggling slightly, she managed to remove herself from the chair. She thanked them both for their time, and left the meeting room. Her mother appeared annoyed at the length of time spent away from her snooping ears.

"Did you tell them how much you hate me?" she asked sarcastically.

Caroline rolled her eyes and silently walked past her and out the office door. She stood by the family car, her back stiff, while she waited impatiently for her mother to unlock the door.

"Some serious dysfunction there," Jennifer said to Simone, as they watched through the window as the two angry women exited the parking lot.

Thirteen

Rehabilitation for the broken metatarsal bone in Jennifer's foot required walking at least half a mile twice a day. She had worn spike heels for decades, which shortened her Achilles tendon. Since the break, she has had to learn how to navigate level ground again, which caused pain and excruciating spasms when the muscles were stretched. It took months of intense and painful physical therapy, exercises, and various shoe heights to get her arches to feel comfortable, and readjust to wearing sneakers. Her foot was now close to being completely healed. She started out slowly, going to the mailbox. Gradually, she achieved going around the block, and now she was able to manage a mile. She longed for the day when she'd be able to wear her trademark 6" heels again.

Jennifer and Goober often strolled the boardwalk at Silver Sands Park in Milford, Connecticut, which wasn't too far from where she lived. Depending on the tide, she and her fiancé, Anthony Palmieri would meet at the beginning of the tombolo leading to Charles Island, and go out to the island, where they would make love. It was here that Anthony left Jennifer to die from the elements. The incoming tides were ferocious, and many people had drowned trying to get back to shore. She had known not to try to attempt this feat. Luckily, some people, out on a sail, were anchored nearby, and heard her cries as she ran towards them screaming for help. That was when Jennifer fell and was severely injured.

One hot afternoon in July, after rambling for thirty minutes, she rested on a bench with Charles Island in sight. Goober sat at her feet, frequently emitting a growl when a seagull landed nearby, taunting the dog into a game of chase. The bird cawed at Goober as if to say, "Catch me if you can. Nah, nah, nah." Jennifer's eyes closed, and the nightmare of being left alone on Charles Island resurfaced. She twitched slightly, and let out a moan. Goober began to bark, waking her from the dream. She rubbed his head, and assured him she was fine. "Only a bad dream, Goobs. All gone, now. Good boy."

But her eyes quickly closed again. And this time, she fell into a deep slumber. She dreamt about the last appointment she had with Dr. Michael Brady, the attending orthopedist at Yale-New Haven Hospital, where she was brought after she was rescued by the Coast Guard.

That's when Dr. Brady presented the news:

"You cannot wear stiletto heels any longer."

"But I've worn high heels since I was a teenager," Jennifer countered.

"You'll just have to adjust. Your tendons shrunk, and it will take more physical therapy and regular exercise to stop your calves and feet from going into spasm," he reiterated.

"I don't want people to know how short I really am," Jennifer quipped, trying to make a joke out of her situation.

Dr. Brady said with slight flirtation in his voice, "You know, good things come in small packages."

Jennifer looked closely at the doctor's face. She could not pull her gaze away. His eyes were filled with amusement, enhanced by the hint of crow's feet in the corners. His smile, a backdrop for his perfectly whitened teeth, was warm and welcoming. It took a great deal of self-control for Jennifer not to run her fingers through his thick, black, wavy hair.

They both had the same cobalt blue eyes. Jennifer was often complimented on her eyes, mostly by men. This time she felt she was looking into a mirror, except there was a handsome, stubble-bearded face looking back at her. She felt she could stare into Michael Brady's eyes for hours, like opposite magnetic forces pulling each other together.

"Ahem," the doctor said, breaking the moment. "I'll see you next month. Actually, my associate will be seeing you. I'm going to another hospital for two months, as part of a training program for the newly graduated interns."

"Oh no," Jennifer blurted out, expressing disappointment. Catching herself she added, "I mean, that's a promotion for you, I assume."

The doctor nodded. As he jotted down notes on his tablet, Jennifer observed a slight grin forming in the corners of his mouth. He stopped writing, looked at Jennifer and hesitated before speaking. "I'll be at St. Raphael's Hospital. Just down the road." He removed a business card from his pocket, turned it over, and quickly wrote something down. He handed the card to Jennifer and said in a low, almost sultry voice, *"Call me anytime if you have a setback. I'll get you to a specialist, without having to wait weeks for an appointment."*

Jennifer took the card and slipped it into her purse. They shook hands, Jennifer wanting to hold his hand forever.

"Thank you," she whispered.

"My pleasure. I hope to see you again, wearing flats, and minus the cane."

Simone was in the waiting room; Jennifer's ride to and from the appointment. As the two women were about to leave the reception area, a voice broke out. "Take care of those feet." They turned to see Dr. Brady's wide smile, his eyes clearly intimating 'call me, Jennifer.'

Smiling back, she turned and headed towards Simone's car.

Goober jumped in the back seat, and Simone latched his doggie seat belt around him. Jennifer sat in the front staring out the window as if willing Dr. Brady to come flying out the door, rushing to her and asking her to stay.

"I maintain that man has an obvious crush on you," Simone said.

There was no response. "Jennifer? Earth to Jennifer."

Jennifer turned toward Simone. "Oh, sorry. I was daydreaming. He really is a nice doctor, don't you think?"

"Nice? That's what you call him – nice? He's gorgeous, Jennifer. And he likes you. It's written all over his fetching flirtatious face."

"Yes . . . nice . . . very nice . . ."

Jennifer was talking in her sleep, alerting Goober to her increased anxiety. The dog began barking and pushed at her hand, waking Jennifer from her dream.

"Wow, Goober, that dream seemed so real. We need to go home," she said petting him under his collar. Goober trotted next to Jennifer as they walked along the boardwalk heading toward her cottage.

Fourteen

September 2019

After her meeting with Simone and Jennifer, Caroline felt invigorated. Finally, she had met two women who understood her, didn't mock her, and who wanted to help. Simone was correct: the more Caroline ate, the more weight she gained, causing her to descend into a downward spiral. It was a self-defeating cycle.

Caroline made up her mind that she was going to seriously work on losing weight. Her Aunt Adele had said she was willing to help in any way she could, and Caroline would take her up on her offer.

"Aunt Adele, can we get together tomorrow afternoon? I have a few things to discuss."

"Sure," her aunt said. "Is anything wrong?"

"No, quite the opposite."

"Want to meet at the new fondue place in Nyack, by the water? The water views are lovely," Adele asked.

"Actually, I'd prefer not to go to a restaurant. I'd rather we meet at a park bench by the dock. Maybe we can grab a bite afterwards, but I don't want others overhearing our conversation. I'll see you there at ten," Caroline said with some authority, and she hung up.

Adele was curious about what Caroline wanted to discuss, and why they couldn't meet at the restaurant.

Her anxiety increased, hoping Caroline wouldn't broach the subject of who was her biological mother. *Maybe Evelyn told her,* Adele mused. She decided not to allow these thoughts to take over. She had papers to grade, and she needed to focus on the task at hand. Tomorrow would come soon enough to discover what Caroline had on her mind.

At precisely ten o'clock, Adele found Caroline sitting on the bench, scribbling in a notebook.

"I must say, Caroline, you've roused my curiosity." She looked down at the notebook, which Caroline quickly stashed inside her purse. "Are you sure everything is, okay?"

"Everything is perfect, Aunt Adele. Just perfect. I wanted to tell you that I've come to three major decisions."

Adele geared herself for Caroline's proclamation.

"First," Caroline announced, "I'm going on a diet. I know I've said this before, but now I'm *really* going to lose weight, and I need your help. You had offered to go to *Overeaters Anonymous* with me. Are you still agreeable to that?"

"Of course," Adele said with great relief. "Anytime. I'd be happy to go with you. But the meetings are here in Nyack, and you live in Mt. Vernon, forty minutes away."

Caroline abruptly interrupted. "That brings me to topic number two," she said. "I'm going to look for an apartment in Nyack. I love this town, and I love you. It's time for me to leave the nest and go out on my own. So, if you don't mind, I'd like to look for a rental . . . today . . . if you'd come with me."

"Of course," Adele said, admiringly. "Absolutely." She paused for a moment, hoping number three wasn't leaving her sister's home because the secret was out. Adele composed herself and meekly asked, "And number three?"

"I'm getting married."

"What!" Adele almost screamed. "Married? To whom?" The questions were now flying out of her aunt's mouth . . . "Who is he? When? What do your parents think?"

Caroline put up her hand to stop the inquiries.

"I'm marrying myself," she said confidently and with great determination.

Adele was speechless.

"My mother and I met with wedding planners in Fairfield, Connecticut to discuss it all. Let's face it, Aunt Adele, no one is going to want to marry me. I'm fat, ugly and I'm getting older. I'll never meet a man, and I'll never have kids."

Adele's eyes teared. "Please don't say that, Caroline. You're a beautiful woman, and any man would be crazy not to love you."

Caroline raised her hand again. She had to remain firm, and didn't want her aunt to infuse her mind with questions. "I'm going to marry myself, Aunt Adele. And I want you to be there as my witness."

Adele put her hand on her chest, as if the words were bricks tumbling down upon her. "Your mother knows about this?" she asked. "She's okay with this?"

"No. You know how my mother is. Anything I do is never good enough for her. Only Wanda can do no wrong. They paid for Wanda's wedding. Afterwards, Mom assured me there was money for my wedding, too. I think she said that simply because she knew that would never happen. So, I'm going to have the wedding of my dreams, and they can pay for it."

Adele took some time to process it all. Caroline sounded more like a spoiled brat, demanding what she felt she was entitled to, which was so alien to Adele's way of thinking.

"It all sounds . . .well . . . a bit different," Adele feigned interest. "When, and where are you having the wedding?"

"Next March in Miami," she blurted out quickly.

Miami. The word hit Adele hard. Memories came flooding back of that fateful day in the attic and Marcelo. What were the odds that Caroline, or she, would run into him? He must be in his mid-seventies by now, she calculated. He was almost twice her age . . . she wondered what he looked like . . . was he still married . . . did he even remember her? Her fantasies were spinning out of control.

"Aunt Adele?" Caroline interrupted her reverie. "So, what do you think?"

"Well, I think it's an interesting concept," Adele said. "I've never heard of anyone marrying themselves. What did your parents say when you told them?"

"They hate the idea. My mother said she and daddy aren't coming, and she's going to call all our relatives in Florida and tell them not to attend."

"Why Miami?" Adele asked, afraid of the answer.

"I thought it would be more convenient for our relatives. Besides, I'd like to get away to a warm destination for a few weeks. So, auntie? Will you come?"

Adele pushed away her anxiety. "Yes, of course, Caroline. I'll be there, and I'm happy to be your witness, though, this will take some time to digest."

"Thank you, Aunt Adele. I knew I could count on your support," Caroline said. "I have a lot of details to work out, but I feel good about my decisions. Speaking of which, let's go apartment hunting."

The two women stepped into a real estate office on Main Street. An agent took down Caroline's information. Fortunately, she had a few free hours so she took them to see six apartments. By two o'clock, Caroline had signed a lease for a three-bedroom apartment overlooking the Hudson River. It was a fourth-floor walk-up, which she welcomed as an opportunity for forced exercise. Afterwards, the women stopped for lunch, trying out the new fondue restaurant.

When she left her aunt that day, Caroline was ecstatic, with a firm and positive direction to her life. Adele left with a heavy heart, with memories of Marcelo, and the fear of Caroline one day discovering the truth.

Fifteen

A meeting was scheduled with Caroline Wight for Monday November twenty-fifth at eleven o'clock. It had been over two months since Simone and Jennifer had seen her. After initial greetings, Caroline gushed, "I've lost twenty-two pounds! And Aunt Adele lost fifteen. I've learned that it doesn't take a long time for fat to come on, but it takes a long time for it to go. It's a hard journey, ladies, but one I'm willing to take."

"That's wonderful news, Caroline," Jennifer said.

"We are very happy for you," Simone added.

"There's an *Overeaters Anonymous* group at Aunt Adele's church. I know that I'm not alone. Many turn to food when they're sad, happy, lonely, or just for the hell of it. I'm viewing life differently now. Last month I moved into my own apartment, a few miles from my aunt. It's time I take responsibility for my life."

My goodness," Simone said, joyously. "I'm so happy for you . . . *sincerely* happy," she reiterated.

"Me, too," Jennifer said. "So much has happened since we first met."

"I feel like a new woman. And, I have you two to thank." Caroline continued, "You opened my eyes to how self-destructive I was. I knew I was hurting no one but myself, especially by closet eating. My therapist has been a huge support, too."

"A therapist?" Jennifer appeared surprised. "So, you did listen to our suggestions."

"It took a lot to make the initial phone call, but once I met with her and started talking, a lot of past demons surfaced, which I had kept suppressed for years. I'm excited about my new outlook."

"Good for you. Getting started is half the battle," Jennifer said.

"I even decided to have a funeral for my junk food," Caroline said, a hint of excitement in her voice, hoping the two would ask for more information.

"A *what?*" Simone asked. She looked shocked.

"Yes, a food funeral," Caroline reiterated. "I know you're going to think this is as kooky as marrying myself, but I'm going to have a funeral for all the candy bars, bags of snacks, and cookies hidden in my apartment and in my car. Only Aunt Adele understands. I haven't told my parents, because I know they'll think it's another weird addition to my bizarre persona. She and I are going to dig a hole in her backyard and bury all the forbidden foods. The sweets will be dead to me, never to enter my life again."

"I don't know what to say," Jennifer remarked. "I've never heard of such a thing. Pretty smart, if you can emotionally separate yourself from the treats."

"In the future, I'll look at candy bars, and bags of chips, cookies and pretzels as foods I'm allergic to, that will make me violently ill. They'll be like the negative people in my life who don't serve me well."

"You're sounding so strong," Simone said. "You're on the right path, Caroline."

"I'm going to have to stay strong, especially this week, now that Thanksgiving is only a few days away. Aunt Adele and I have our meal plans set. We're going to weigh our food at the table. That'll show my mother that I can do this."

Simone and Jennifer remained silent. It seemed obvious Caroline was still angry at her mother for the way her life had turned out.

"How *is* your mother taking to the new you?" ask Simone, fearing this would open Pandora's Box.

"She wasn't at all supportive. She doesn't believe I'll stick with the diet . . . that it's just a phase . . . that in time, I'll go back to my old ways. But the more she puts me down, the more determined I've become," Caroline said with conviction. "She's not coming to Florida to see me 'make a fool of myself,' nor is she going to give me any money towards the wedding. It's going to be very small; maybe twenty people. She told her family that I lost my mind, and that they should not support my craziness by attending. She told them that she and my daddy aren't going, so why should they? The more I talked about my wedding, the more stubborn I became. She's so . . ."

Simone cut off Caroline's rant. She realized that she should not have asked about the mother. It was a mistake she now regretted. She got the conversation back on track.

"From what you just told us do you still want to marry yourself?" Simone asked.

"Yes, I do, more than ever. I'm learning to love myself now, and I promise to take care of my body going forward."

"Have you discussed the wedding ceremony with your therapist?"

"Yes." Caroline became pensive, and suddenly silent.

Simone sensed this was a subject Caroline wasn't yet willing to discuss. She put her finger to her lips, gesturing to Jennifer: 'don't ask'. "So Caroline, have you decided when and where you want the wedding?"

"I'm planning the wedding for March 2020 in Key Biscayne. By then, I will have lost more weight, and it will be before my snowbird relatives leave Florida to return north."

"Jennifer will be working directly with you, Caroline, as I'm on maternity leave for several months," Simone said, trying to bring the meeting to a conclusion. "I'd suggest you come back to the office later this week, to sign a contract, leave a deposit, and go over more of your ideas with Jennifer."

"I can come this Friday, if that works for you."

"Yes, that's fine," Jennifer said. "I have an opening at ten o'clock."

Simone added, "Meanwhile, we'll do research on venues and ceremony ideas."

The conversation left Simone ruminating. Caroline's life was so unlike her own. A sologamy wedding, a funeral for food . . . what's next?

Sixteen

Simone and Jennifer discussed how they could help Caroline accomplish a non-traditional wedding without too many expenses or complications. A few times, Simone had paid the wedding expenses for a couple in-need. Often, she had absorbed the cost for everything, including a honeymoon. It was her way of giving back. She was very fortunate to have a successful business, and she knew there were many who could not afford to pay hundreds of thousands on their wedding.

Several years ago, Simone met a woman who was dying of cancer. It was her wish to marry the man she loved. With the help of Charlie Hamilton, whom Simone hardly knew at the time, she provided a wonderful wedding for the couple, including a weekend away in the Berkshires. The woman died three months later. She had written a touching letter to Simone, thanking her for making her feel happy and healthy during her final days.

Simone decided she would give Caroline some extra perks for signing a contract with "I Do". She wasn't going to do the wedding for free, as she still had to pay Jennifer a salary, plus other expenses. But she would figure out something.

At the Friday meeting, Jennifer went over the details of the contract with Caroline, and explained how Simone wanted to help her financially. Caroline graciously accepted.

Jennifer stood up, to signal the meeting was over, when she asked, "How are things with your family?"

"My parents are definitely not coming," Caroline said, sadly. "Aunt Adele said she'll be there, although my mother is mad at her for supporting me."

Jennifer sensed a deep sadness in her voice, and knew Caroline could spend all day talking to her. Planning her wedding was one thing, but Jennifer was not trained to take on family problems. Jennifer opened the conference room door and wished her well. "I'll be in touch next week," she promised.

Caroline faced a forty-five-minute drive back to her apartment. To pass the time, she decided to call Wanda, and ask her to be part of her bridal party. As usual, Wanda seemed distracted and disinterested in hearing what her sister had to say.

"I asked Aunt Adele to give me away, and to be my maid of honor. Can you be a bridesmaid? You can wear anything you want. You don't need to purchase anything special."

"Good," said Wanda, pausing to light a cigarette and taking a deep drag, "because I don't want to put out any extra money if I don't have to. You know, Caroline, I agree with mom and dad. This is a stupid idea. You're forcing my family and me to go to Florida – not to mention the relatives who said they'd show up. Do you think I'm made of money? This will be a big financial strain on us."

"But you said you were going to spend several days at Disney World. That you can afford? How about you skip my wedding, Wanda?" said Caroline, her anger rising. "Mom and Dad don't want to come, so I'm not surprised you don't want to, either."

"They don't want to go because they think it's an embarrassment," Wanda said, in between taking deep pulls on her cigarette.

"You mean, they think *I'm* an embarrassment."

"You said it, not me. I'm your only ally, Caroline. I'm the one who told them to take you in."

Caroline was so enraged; she didn't hear what her sister had just said. She retorted, "I've had to put up with a lot of your crap while growing up, Wanda. I don't need, or want, any more of it. So just stay home with your egotistical husband and bratty daughter, Stella." Caroline surprised herself at how strong she sounded. She felt suddenly empowered, ready to take on anyone who insulted her.

"How dare you say that to me? You don't know anything about my husband, and Stella is just a little kid. A child . . . something you'll *never* have."

"I'm hanging up now, Wanda. Good bye." Caroline put down the phone, taking a deep cleansing breath. But a familiar inner turmoil began to rise. It was a feeling of losing control, a yearning, and a need for something to kill the emotions boiling inside of her. What she craved more than anything was feelings of comfort, love, and support. "No!" she screamed aloud as she drove over the bridge connecting Westchester County to Nyack.

Tears streamed down Caroline's face, dripping off her chin and onto her blouse. Her mind was racing, her heart pounding.

She got off her exit, pulled to the side of the road, and sobbed. She felt there was something . . . a deep secret . . . that no one wanted her to know. She lifted the armrest of her car, and stared at a bright yellow bag of peanut M&M's. As her hand reached for the bag, she realized that the logo upside down looked like W&W. *Weight Watchers.* As if the bag were on fire, she withdrew her hand. "No," she repeated aloud, "I am not going to give into your temptation." She rolled down the window, and quickly tossed the bag out onto the grass. "You will never tempt me again. I am strong. I don't need you to validate my happiness." Anyone watching her would think she was a kook for yelling at a bag of candy.

She pulled away from the spot and drove the rest of the way to her apartment, feeling proud of her newly-found self-control. She called her Aunt Adele, who was her support partner in the weight loss program. She told her about her conversation with Wanda, and how she had tossed the bag of candy out the window.

"I'm so proud of you, Caroline," her aunt gushed. "You've come a long way." After a pensive moment, she added, "Caroline, don't let Wanda upset you. She's jealous."

"Jealous?" Caroline asked. "How could she be jealous of me?"

"Think about it. You're living in your own apartment. You are free to come and go, and do whatever you please. Wanda went from living with your parents to being a married woman, and now a mother. She never had the opportunity to grow into her own woman. Now, you're getting married, and won't have to answer to any man. Maybe she feels trapped, and unhappy. Yes, I think she's jealous of you, Caroline."

Caroline could not comprehend that Wanda, or anyone else for that matter, could be jealous of her. Caroline was the one who was always jealous of others.

She reminisced about her days in grammar and high school. Those girls were skinnier, prettier, and had more possessions than she. Her classmates got new outfits for the beginning of the school year and for the holidays. Caroline had to shop in the big-girl department, and her clothes were either dark brown or gray. "You need to hide your fat," her mother would say in the dressing room.

The only thing Caroline had, that the other girls didn't have: a secret stash of candy. "I bet Sally McClusky would be jealous if she saw my pile of Milky Way bars," Caroline would say as she sat in her closet, consuming her fifth candy.

But now, years later, Aunt Adele thinks someone is jealous of me? Could it be possible?

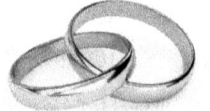

Seventeen

Jennifer did her research on venues willing to do the wedding. The hardest person to secure was a justice of the peace. "A mockery of the sacrament of marriage," said one JP, although he had advertised performing non-religious ceremonies. He chastised Jennifer for making such a request that went against the beliefs of God Almighty. She apologized for taking up his time, and hung up. It took seven calls before she found a JP who understood Caroline's thinking. "I dig it," he said. "It'll be cool."

The wedding was going to be a morning ceremony from nine to eleven. Simple, sweet, and not infringing on people's time. The caterer didn't have a problem accommodating Caroline's request for a breakfast buffet: a variety of bite-size quiches, mini muffins, custom-made omelets, cheese platters, bagels and cream cheese, smoked salmon, breakfast sausages, parfait glasses of yogurt, and large baskets of muffins and scones. Completing this sumptuous smorgasbord of goodies would be large bowls of fresh fruits.

Beverages included mimosas, prosecco, various juices, coffee and tea. The final menu would be finalized several days before the wedding when Caroline and Jennifer were in Florida.

Round 60" tables with simple white linen tablecloths and starched white napkins would be placed around the room. Since her guest list included thirty-five people, Jennifer designed six tables, with six guests at each table. The centerpieces would consist of lavish displays of seasonal flowers. Nothing extravagant, ostentatious, or expensive. Just tasteful and elegant in their simplicity.

The pièce de résistance would be a large four-layer artificial cake. She did not want a topper; only fresh flowers cascading down one side. Caroline preferred fresh fruit for dessert. Jennifer and Simone had planned a wedding ten years before, which had also included a custom-made artificial cake. The "real" one – a sheet cake was stored in the kitchen. It saved the couple thousands of dollars, and no one knew the difference.

Caroline contracted the DJ to play music from the '80s and '90s, with a few Big Band era tunes mixed in for the older generation. She appropriately requested, "I Am Woman" as Adele escorted her down the aisle. If Wanda showed up, she'd be the other witness. If not, Jennifer agreed to step in.

All the contracted vendors, progressive and liberal, were excited to participate in such an unconventional wedding, Even the photographer told them he was a "hip and open-minded millennial." All contracts were signed, deposits made, and the wedding was planned for March 21, 2020.

Eighteen

There were news reports of the COVID-19 virus spreading throughout several states, including Florida. Simone and Jennifer were closely tracking them all. Florida had fifty cases as of March 13th, though no reported cases on Key Biscayne. Jennifer and Caroline were flying out the next day, and by then cases in Florida had skyrocketed to one hundred fifteen. Disney World announced they were shutting down as of March 15th, the height of spring vacation.

The two women were anxious, but were assured by the airline that their flight was scheduled to depart on time. The plane was fairly empty, with only four other people in first class. Jennifer promised Simone that if cases of the virus grew, she and Caroline would be on the first flight back to Connecticut.

On March 14th, the two women and two dogs flew to Florida to take care any of any last-minute items. One of the perks Simone provided for Caroline and the dogs was first class tickets to Florida. Pyewacket fit neatly inside a bag under Caroline's seat. Goober had his own seat, looking out the window as houses grew smaller and smaller as the plane ascended. If possible, he would have stuck his head out the small window with his tongue flying in the wind.

Jennifer and Caroline, both needing vacation time, would spend a few days on the beach. Caroline wanted to get away from the stress of the wedding, and Jennifer needed to spend time away from the chill of the northeast winter.

Jennifer rented a car at the Miami Airport, and the ladies and their respective pooches drove to Key Biscayne, where they checked into their oceanfront rooms at the Ritz Carlton Key Biscayne. Jennifer arranged meetings with the vendors, finalizing the details. The Key Biscayne Beach Club promised to provide a memorable event with all the proper amenities.

Wanda and her family kept their plans for Disney World. They flew down on the thirteenth, and upon check-in were told that Disney World was closing down in two days. Until then, they were welcome to stay at the hotel and enjoy the amenities. If they wished to check out sooner, they would not be charged after the fifteenth.

"I'm not concerned about the virus," Wanda told her mother when she called to say they had arrived. Evelyn had tried to discourage her daughter from going to Disney World, and especially to Caroline's wedding. But to no avail.

"The news reports are saying cases in Florida are rising daily," Evelyn said.

"Haven't you heard, it's a hoax?" Wanda refuted.

Nothing could stop Wanda from enjoying this vacation. She had paid for it, and deserved time away. She had scheduled a body scrub, a massage, a facial, a mani-cure, and pedicure. There wasn't anything that was going to keep her away. Her husband, Brian, could take Stella to the Magic Kingdom, while she enjoyed a day of beauty.

Meanwhile, Caroline's phone rang non-stop from the minute she entered her room. Each call was from a different relative, acknowledging their regrets.

"I'm so sorry dear," Aunt Joan said. "Your uncle and I cannot make it to the wedding. We're too afraid to travel. I'm sure you understand. Send us photos . . ."

"Caroline, we are sorry. But your Aunt Barbara and I can't afford to risk our health. She's got COPD . . ."

"Hello, dear. We feel terrible, but this virus frightens us . . ."

By the end of the day, every guest had canceled.

After speaking to her mother, Wanda called Caroline.

"We just arrived at the hotel and we were told that Disney is closing on Sunday. So, we are heading down to Key Biscayne to spend the week there until your wedding. What a pain in the ass this has become."

"I'm sorry your plans have changed, Wanda."

"It's all your fault." Wanda snarled. "If you hadn't come up with this stupid idea, we wouldn't have come down to Florida in the first place."

Caroline kept her composure and remained mute. She could hear her sister puffing away on a cigarette. "The virus is not my fault, Wanda. How do you think I feel that my plans might have to be changed?"

"I can't worry about your plans, Caroline. I have to think about my family. If this virus hits Key Biscayne, we're taking the first flight out. And God help you if we get sick. You, and your stupid ideas."

Caroline had not told her sister that very few people would be in attendance. At that moment she hated her sister, and she didn't care if she was annoyed. Wanda didn't care about her, so why should she worry how she felt?

The next call was the most painful for Caroline. "Aunt Adele, don't come. The coronavirus is raging. Cancel your flight immediately. I'll reimburse you if the airline doesn't, though I'm sure they will give you a credit. No one is coming, so I'm not having the ceremony. Jennifer and I are going to return home as soon as we can get everything taken care of and canceled.

The two spoke for over an hour. Adele spent most of the time consoling her niece. "Just try to stay strong. The stress can easily cause your diet to backfire. If you need to talk, call me anytime."

"Thank you, Aunt Adele. So far, I'm doing okay, though I will admit, I've been tempted to eat everything in the mini bar. I finally asked the hotel to remove everything, except the water."

"You're amazing, Caroline," her aunt said encouragingly. "If you can get through all of this without overeating, you'll be able to handle anything."

Later that afternoon, Caroline and Jennifer met at the pool bar, where they ordered sparkling water and a vegetable crudité.

Caroline told Jennifer about her aunt. "Since I can remember, Adele has always been there for me,

Jennifer. She babysat when my parents went out. She'd even accompany us to Florida on vacations, and she comes to our home for breakfast every Sunday."

"She sounds like a wonderful woman," Jennifer agreed. "Does she have a family of her own?"

"No, she never married. No children. I've heard whisperings that she once had a boyfriend who broke her heart. But any time I ask my mother about him, she tells me to mind my own business, and to never ask her sister about this. So, I never did."

"What does Adele do for a living?"

"She's the Superintendent of Schools in Nyack, New York. She must do very well because she has a big home furnished with antiques, and she goes on exotic vacations with her friends, including cruises around the world."

"She sounds well-traveled and educated."

"She is. She tutored me in math and helped me study for my SAT's." Caroline dug in her purse and pulled out a photo of them standing in front of the New York Public Library.

Jennifer took a second, and then a third look. She noted a strong resemblance, but she said nothing. She had learned her lesson when she once asked a woman when her baby was due, when she wasn't even pregnant.

"She looks like a lovely lady," was all that Jennifer said. "You're lucky to have her in your life, especially since the relationships with your mother and sister seem strained."

"Aunt Adele is the only one who understands me,"

Caroline said, while she stared at the photograph before putting it back in her purse. She suddenly began crying. "I told you, Jennifer, I have bad luck. I can't believe this is happening. The wedding is just days away. And now the virus. What should I do?" she asked.

Jennifer offered no immediate advice. "I have some thoughts, but I need to sort them out, and talk to Simone. You and I are under a lot of stress right now. Let's plan to meet in the morning, after a good night's sleep. We'll have clearer minds then. It'll all work out, Caroline. I guarantee it," Jennifer promised.

No one slept well that night.

Nineteen

March 16, 2020

The women met in the hotel lobby at six o'clock Monday morning, then headed to the shoreline for a walk. It was best to walk before the sun got too hot, or before the end of the day when the mosquitos and no-see-ums attacked. Pye and Goober were on retractable leashes. Every few yards, Goober turned to be sure his mistress was still safe and within range. He sensed the tension. Although there was an illness looming over the entire country, people went about their daily chores and activities. While Jennifer and Caroline strolled, they saw people walking in the distance on the beach, and children playing in the sand.

The newly-formed friendship benefited both women. Caroline encouraged Jennifer to walk an extra half mile, although her arches were craving a rest. Jennifer helped Caroline with her increasing disappointment, and inevitable cancelation of her wedding.

They walked to the end of the wooden slats leading to the sand, and stopped at the flagpole to read the caution sign. Two warning flags waved vigorously on the pole: yellow for medium hazard for surf and currents, and a purple flag for dangerous marine life. A small sign, posted below the flags cautioned that crocodiles resided in the area. The sign had eroded over the years from the wind and sand, and unless one looked very closely at the drawing of the animal, it mimicked two surf boards coming onto shore simultaneously. In the distance was the Cape Florida Lighthouse, built in the 1700s - one of the few remaining lighthouses in the state.

"I wonder how many people actually pay attention to these flags," Jennifer mused. As she looked closer at the small battered sign, she added, "I didn't know there were crocodiles this far north in Florida. I thought they were only in the Everglades or in Tarzan movies."

Caroline responded as the expert she was. "Well, since global warming, the crocodiles, which only lived in warmer climates, emigrated up north following the warming of the cooler waters. They can be found as far north as Sanibel Island, and on the east coast as far up as here in Key Biscayne. There are reports of some even being seen in Palm Beach."

"Wow, I didn't know that. I always thought alligators were the only dangerous reptiles to watch out for," Jennifer said. "How do you know so much about crocodiles, anyway?"

"When I was a child, my parents came down to Everglade City for our Christmas and spring breaks," Caroline explained. "My father's two brothers lived down here all year long. We'd stay with one uncle during Christmas week, and the other uncle during spring break." As Caroline regaled Jennifer with her childhood memories, the two walked onto the sand.

She continued her story. "I'd go exploring with my cousins, and they showed me where crocodiles lived, how to watch out for them, recognize their eggs, and the differences between crocs and alligators. They're fascinating creatures, you know, but you need to stay far away from them. They're fast and stealth-like. Once we took an air boat ride through the Everglades, and you could see crocs lined up in the murky water, just waiting for the boat captain to make a mistake by getting too close to their habitat."

"Do your uncles still live in Florida?" Jennifer asked.

"One uncle passed away several years ago. We stopped coming down when I was eighteen because my father had a fight with one of his brothers. He and his wife had planned to come to the wedding, once they heard my parents weren't attending. The usual family drama. I still have several cousins and an aunt who live in the state. That's one reason why I wanted to have my wedding in Florida: so that my relatives wouldn't use the excuse they couldn't afford to travel up north. But that's a moot point now," Caroline said, sadly. "My mother has done a good job of poisoning the minds of my relatives. And now, the coronavirus."

Once they arrived at the shoreline, they'd let the dogs run and splash in the water. Caroline left behind footprints and memories, washed away with the incoming waves.

The two dogs behaved well around each other. Goober tolerated Pye's annoying insistence of wanting to play. The beach was filling up with walkers, and a few children dug holes in the sand, collecting shells and tiny clams for their plastic buckets.

Caroline squinted as she looked ahead to where Pye and Goober were now frolicking near the water's edge, chasing tiny sea creatures' air bubbles in the mucky sand. Jennifer didn't want to lose sight of Goober, so she called for him to come to her. The beach was growing more crowded, with packs of canines beginning to form, and Jennifer didn't feel easy about the prospect of Goober's herding instinct to surface. He didn't answer her command. Maybe it was the sound of the crashing waves, or his excitement upon meeting a new dog that made him ignore Jennifer. Caroline also spotted Pye in the crowd.

As they continued on, Caroline suddenly blurted out, "Jennifer, I want to marry myself. I feel I've come a very long way since our first meeting. I understand why I was eating so much . . . hiding food in my closet, and ordering food for multiple people. Now I've grown to love and appreciate myself, and I want to follow through with my dream of a wedding, and of eventually, having a child."

All the while the two women kept their eyes on their dogs. Jennifer called Goober again, but he didn't respond. Then she turned to Caroline and said, "I'm still feeling somewhat ambivalent. I find myself deliberating over the idea of a sologamy wedding. I'm struggling to figure out your wishes. On one hand, I understand the dream of having a wedding. I think every little girl dreams of the day she'll walk down the aisle in a beautiful gown, and be the center of attention. Truly, I get it," she said. "But now your parents aren't spending the money they have saved for your wedding, and the idea of having a ceremony just to aggravate your mother is behind you. As Simone pointed out, a light switch isn't going to go on and suddenly life will be different. You're now heading in a wonderful direction with your life. Why not see how things progress, and give yourself a little more time?"

Jennifer paused before continuing. Her strategy was to help Caroline come to a solid decision, almost playing devil's advocate. "Let me ask you this: what if you do marry yourself? Afterwards, you continue to lose weight, build more confidence, and you get your life on the path you desire. What if you meet someone a year or two from now, and fall in love? What if he wants to get married? Do you have to divorce yourself in order to remarry? I mean, is marrying yourself legally binding? Will you have to file for a divorce from yourself?"

"Wow, that's a lot to think about, Jennifer. I never gave it a second thought," Caroline confessed. "I've lived my life without falling in love, I guess I assumed I never would meet a man who would ever want to marry me."

"Just think about the effects of your actions."

After the third call, finally, Goober raced back to Jennifer with Pye trailing behind, looking like a wet rat. The women clipped the leashes on their dog, to prevent them from taking off again, and continued walking for the next fifteen minutes.

"Based on what we've discussed, Caroline, have you made a decision? Are you going to cancel the wedding, or not?"

"Honestly Jennifer," Caroline said. "I'm not ready to make that decision. I'd be disappointed, of course, if I have to abandon the plan. I've looked forward to the day I can celebrate my independence, and my new life. With the virus taking over my plans, I don't know what to do. Should I go through with the ceremony, and have a reception at another time? But then I'd have to come back to Florida, and I don't know if my parents would approve even then. If I do meet someone in the future," Caroline continued, "I'll worry then about undoing my ceremony."

Caroline started a continuous stream of consciousness rant. It was obvious she could not make a decision, and Jennifer knew she had to get her back on track.

"Since you're so uncertain, Caroline," Jennifer interrupted, "how about Simone and I make the decision for you? What do you think about going through with the ceremony two days from now instead of waiting? Your sister and her family will be here by tomorrow, you already have the dress, a cool Justice of the Peace, and a photographer. You can do a simple ceremony. Ask them to take a video to show Aunt Adele, and your parents. That is, if your parents come around to the idea."

Caroline stopped walking and turned to face Jennifer. "You're amazing, you know that?" Caroline said giving Jennifer a hug. "I love the idea."

"I'll call the photographer and the Justice of the Peace to be sure they're available on Wednesday," Jennifer said. "I'll also talk to the hotel banquet manager and explain the change of plans. Don't worry, Caroline, you'll have the wedding of your dreams, even if it's a bit different than planned."

"I knew when I first met you and Simone, that you two would be the perfect planners for me. And I was right. Thank you, Jennifer. I feel reenergized."

"Let's head back to the hotel. I have calls to make, and I'd like to take a nap. Want to meet at 1:30 for lunch?"

"Good idea . . . about the nap, I mean. I didn't sleep either."

Suddenly, they heard people screaming and children crying. A deep growl emanated from Goober's throat. The dog turned towards the water and stood at attention with his tail straight out. His Border Collie instincts kicked into gear. Jennifer stopped, turned to see what caught his attention, and saw the commotion. She knew Goober would charge into action if given the chance. She reached for his collar. Caroline picked up Pye, who wiggled and whimpered in her arms.

People around the water's edge began hollering, some were running back onto the sand, leaving behind their chairs. Children's hands were grabbed by every adult nearby, and brought up to the sand, away from the shoreline. Several men lifted abandoned sand chairs, shells and rocks and starting throwing them at an object close to shore. One man picked up an umbrella, and like a javelin, tossed it into the water.

Back at the water's edge, lifeguards tried to disburse the crowd. A woman screamed, "My baby! My baby!"

Caroline and Jennifer stared at the water. Horror washed over them.

Out of the mucky waters came the body of an enormous crocodile, his mouth opening and closing, attempting to grab one of the toddlers playing on the shoreline. It was rare to see a crocodile in the ocean, especially so far north and so close to the shore. Crocodiles, unlike alligators, have glands which allow them to remove salt from their bodies.

Lifeguards' whistles blew at ear-piercing levels. One ran towards the water with a large stick in his hand. Out of nowhere, police were on the scene. An officer removed his revolver and aimed at the croc. The sound of a loud bang echoed over the water.

A swarm of fifty or so bodies headed towards the narrow path leading up to the beach, in the direction of where Caroline and Jennifer stood with the dogs.

"Run!" yelled Jennifer, as the crowd of people quickly approached them. Pye fell out of Caroline's arms as a group of people en masse pushed her along. She fought her way back toward the beach, calling out for Pye. She followed the sounds of his cries, and found him shaking with fear in the brush filled with twigs, cattails and vines, causing whimpers and minor scratches. She scooped him up, and scurried along with the crowd to the parking lot.

Jennifer fought to keep her balance as she, too, was pushed and shoved. A tall, bulky man, shirtless with an enormously big belly pushed Jennifer so hard that she fell down. As she used her hands to break the fall, the dog's leash released from her hand. Goober took off towards the shoreline.

"Goober!" Jennifer yelled, "Goober, come!"

Meanwhile, Caroline looked around the parking lot, searching for Jennifer. She yelled, "Jennifer! Where are you?"

But Jennifer had returned to the shoreline and was running after Goober. A gripping spasm took hold of her right calf and caused her to fall flat onto the wet sand. Her shoulder slammed into the earthen ground, and she cried out in pain. She raised her head, and saw her dog heading towards the crocodile.

She screamed, "Goober, no!"

Twenty

"Help me, Goober! Help me."

But the dog was running full-speed, charging into the crashing waves. Jennifer feared the worst. "Goober, no . . . no . . ." she sobbed through tears and pain. She cried again, her face becoming streaked with trails of wet sand.

The crocodile was within sight. Standing knee high in the water, policemen and lifeguards were pushed and pulled by the incoming waves, trying to stand their ground in the thick, sucking earth. They took precise aim at the animal, and fired. Its enormous body breached out of the water.

Meanwhile, Goober swam straight for a crying child, only feet from the approaching beast. Without breaking skin, the dog grabbed the toddler by his diaper, lifted him above the water, turned, and carried him back to his wailing mother. Goober resembled a stork delivering a newborn.

Blood pooled and scented the water, as now new and dangerous predators lurked about: sharks. The officers and lifeguards scurried back to the sand. Onlookers stood by, gripped by the fierce water ballet taking place as multiple sharks pounced on the injured crocodile tossing it askew like a chew toy being pulled in every direction.

Frantic mothers were reunited one by one with their missing children; many of whom were scooped up by fellow beach goers. People continued to gather their belongings and run toward the parking lot. Soon, the sound of an approaching police helicopter filled the air. "Clear the beach. Clear the beach," echoed from the aircraft circling above them.

Goober ran to Jennifer and nuzzled her neck. Kneeling in the wet sand, she cried, hugging his wet body. "Oh Goober, I thought I had lost you."

People ran to her, thanking her, and praising her dog's courageous instincts. "A real hero," many acknowledged. "Amazing dog," others added. The mother of the rescued child ran to Jennifer. The baby, still crying, was held close to the woman's breast. "I don't know how to thank you . . . I mean, your dog . . . he's so brave." She bent down and placed a kiss on the dog's wet head. "God bless you," she said. Goober signaled 'you're welcome' by shaking his body dry, and showering all of them with dirty cold water.

Soon, Caroline arrived, with Pye close at foot, his leash firmly attached.

"Are you alright?" she asked Jennifer as she helped her stand up.

"I'm fine." But she really wasn't. Jennifer was shaking. She felt light-headed, and pain was emanating from her ankle and her right shoulder. All she wanted to do was get back to her room.

"Goober was magnificent. He saved that little boy's life," Caroline said.

"Yes, he was a true hero," Jennifer agreed. She picked

up Goober's leash, caked with wet sand, and hobbled back towards the hotel.

Once back in her room, she filled the tub with warm water, and surprisingly, Goober jumped right in. She lathered his coat, rinsed him off, and dried him with a plush hotel bath towel. She showered, and crawled under the covers for a much-welcomed and needed nap. Goober, who usually slept in his travel bed, jumped onto the bed and cuddled next to Jennifer. The two were sound asleep within minutes.

Jennifer awoke to the sound of her phone's alarm. For a moment, she had forgotten where she was, or the day and time. The room, streamed with daylight, added to her disorientation. But her sore ankle and shoulder jolted her memory back to the events of that morning.

She contacted the vendors and discussed the change of plans. Then, she called Simone and brought her up to date on Caroline's decision to go through with the ceremony, which was now scheduled to take place in two days. Lastly, she filled her in on the horrific adventures involving Goober, the child, and the crocodile.

"Are you okay?" Simone asked, alarmed.

"I think I reinjured my ankle. My shoulder is bruised, but otherwise, I'm fine. I got so frightened when I saw Goober charging into the water to save the child."

"Where was the mother? Weren't there other people around?" Simone asked.

Jennifer wondered the same thing. "I guess everyone was so focused on the crocodile, that no one noticed the toddler being pushed down by the waves. Simone, people were screaming and running about. It was utter chaos."

"You know what this all means, don't you?" Simone asked Jennifer. "You'll have to go back to see Dr. Brady again."

Jennifer chuckled. "You're so wicked, Simone."

While Jennifer rode the elevator down to the lobby, she thought about Dr. Brady gently examining her injured ankle. A smile crossed her face as she stepped off the lift, and saw Caroline, looking equally refreshed.

Jennifer updated her on her conversations with the vendors; all agreeing to cancel without charge. The Justice of the Peace and the photographer were available on Wednesday at nine o'clock.

The photographer suggested they meet a few minutes earlier, at the hotel's private walkway over by the marsh. There, he planned to take some still photos before the ceremony. "Be sure your entire family is present. We don't want to forget anyone."

"My entire family," Caroline repeated to Jennifer. "What a joke. The biggest day of my life, and the only family member in attendance will be my sister."

"You need to focus on yourself," Jennifer said. "Don't let outside intrusions ruin the day." She hoped Caroline would heed her advice.

Twenty One

Simone's anxiety over the coronavirus mounted. She feared for her family's health, and that of Mrs. Smith, who was sixty-eight, and Irene, who was seventy. It seemed as if overnight, everyone's lives had changed. Stores, schools, businesses, churches and restaurants closed down. People were having fist fights over toilet paper. Others hoarded disinfectant wipes, paper towels, and other supplies. Small bottles of hand sanitizers were being sold online for five times their cost. Mandates to wear face masks went into effect. People stood six feet apart, families no longer got together, and rising unrest became the norm.

Business at the Grand Hamilton Hotel, owned and operated by Charlie's family, came to a screeching halt. Conferences, weddings, events, and hotel room bookings were canceled. The lobby, usually overflowing with incoming guests and hotel staff, was barren. An emergency meeting was held in mid-March, when Charlie's father announced the hotel would close down for at least six weeks, or until the height of the virus had, hopefully, passed. The staff was put on standby, with the confidence that soon this crisis would end.

Charlie set up his office at home. He spent his days reading news reports, and speaking to other hotel managers across the country, and throughout Europe. Everyone was feeling the effects of the global outbreak, and the Grand Hamilton Hotel was not immune.

Immediately after the lockdown was announced, the four adults sat down and came up with a plan of action. Charlie was in charge of ordering food for the two households. No one was to go into a supermarket or drug store. He would have all the food delivered to their homes. Everything was sterilized with wipes, and left to air dry, including the daily mail.

Mrs. Smith and Irene would be the only people permitted to come in contact with Charlie, Simone and the babies, and vice versa. As soon as anyone stepped outside, they'd have to don masks, and immediately wash their hands upon entering each other's homes, especially before handling the babies.

For weeks, Simone, Charlie, Mrs. Smith and Irene followed this routine and protocol. Their hands were raw from frequent washing and sanitizers. The news around the country grew increasingly grim, mostly in New York City, where each day thousands were dying or becoming infected.

Many people with second homes in Westport stopped coming up only on weekends. Instead, they left their city apartments and moved permanently into their safer suburban sanctuaries. There, they didn't have to worry about crowded elevators, pushing buttons or doors, or having to avoid neighbors. Their mail was forwarded, their lights shut off, and their apartment doors were locked behind them.

"You look worried," Simone said to her husband, as he focused on a computer Excel spreadsheet.

"I *am* worried," he admitted. "I know you and I will be fine, but I'm concerned about the staff. Many have young families to feed, and bills to pay. In a way, Simone, I'm feeling guilty for being able to afford living in our beautiful home, and not feeling anxious over finances. There's got to be something we can do."

"There is," Simone agreed. "Let's set up a fund for the employees. Keep them on full salary for the next six to eight weeks, with the understanding they'll return to the hotel once it is up and operational. Ask your father how much money he's willing to dole out to support his staff, many of whom have been with the hotel for decades."

"But what if this virus goes on for six months or longer?" Charlie asked. "We don't have the hotel capital to keep employees on the payroll that long. There's talk about a stimulus package being considered and voted on. That will help. Maybe the workers will receive some government support by way of unemployment checks."

"You can't take on the troubles of the world, Charlie," Simone said as she put her arms around him. "But we can and should do what we can. It is times like these when people like us can have the most impact on others."

"What do you mean?" Charlie asked.

"First, we can make substantial donations to the food banks. I think those affected will struggle to feed their families. I, too, have to close my office, but I'll pay my employees until things turn around. If I have to use up this year's funds from my trust account, I will. I've been reading about meetings taking place online. Why not stream events or conferences? If a couple wants to get married, they can."

"But how will you make money, Simone? People aren't going to pay your going rate to link them up on the Internet."

"No, they won't, and I wouldn't expect them to pay an exorbitant amount just to say they had an "I Do" wedding. But I'd help them plan their wedding for a minimum fee, or even, in some cases, pro bono. I can create ways for couples to rethink their wedding, breaking it down into three categories: splurge, spend or save."

"That sounds intriguing," Charlie said. "Give me an example."

Simone loved brainstorming with Charlie. Often a man's point of view was radically different than a woman's, for example, Jennifer's. She continued, "Let's say the couple wants to keep their existing budget, but their number of guests has decreased to a gathering of twenty people. Instead of being conservative with their menu, they can now serve higher priced foods, such as caviar, sushi, paté, lobster, filet mignon or Veuve Clicquot champagne. That is if they still have the funds, and are secure in their jobs. Simone continued, "Otherwise, if they've lost their jobs and now need to cut their budget to a bare minimum, I can make suggestions. Such as, the bride can look for a dress in a consignment shop or Goodwill, they can do a light breakfast instead of a sit-down dinner, and they can serve house champagne. The centerpieces can be dessert. The bride can rent jewelry and the dress. And they can postpone the honeymoon until they're back to work. There are lots of ways to create a wedding without breaking the bank."

"Don't you normally do this sort of budgeting suggestions with the couples?" Charlie asked.

"Not often. Remember, the couples I work with usually have an over-the-top budget, and they don't want to hear how they can shave off a few bucks here and there."

Simone's mind began racing with ideas. "I need to create an outline of the consulting program. I want to run these ideas past Jennifer, and between the two of us I'm sure we can come up with a plan." She paused the conversation when she heard cries from the nursery. She rushed off to take care of the newborns, whom every passing day were becoming little people with distinct personalities.

Simone leaned over Henry's and Maggie's cribs. "What sort of world will you be living in, my little darlings?" she whispered. "I fear your future might never know the same freedom and peace your father and I have enjoyed during our lifetimes."

She thought back to the New Year's Eve party at the Grand Hamilton Hotel over a year ago, when the G-men stood off in a corner whispering. *Did they know then what was in store for our country, and the world? Were they warned about the dangers of this virus, and kept it a secret?*

Twenty-Two

Simone, Charlie, Mrs. Smith, and Irene sat around the dining room table. Although they were the only people who had come in contact with each other, they kept their distance.

"Simone, Irene and I are considering returning to Charlottesville," Mrs. Smith announced. "I spoke to Judy, who said, though there aren't many cases of the virus in the Charlottesville area, they are escalating where she lives in Richmond, so they're both teaching virtually from home. Besides, there are other reasons I should go back to Virginia."

She continued, "I don't want to get infected and bring it back to you, or to the babies. I would never forgive myself. Or to you, Irene," she said, reaching for the woman's hand. I miss my home. I couldn't stay in the lovely house next door . . . I miss Henry . . ." her voice trailed off, as she searched her purse for a tissue. "I'm sorry, Simone, but I think I should go back to Virginia."

Simone looked at Charlie for an answer, or, at least, some support. But he was as shocked by this announcement as was his wife. "I don't know how to advise you, Mrs. Smith," Simone said. "You have to do what makes you feel comfortable. Your safety, and Irene's, is what's most important."

"If one of you," Charlie added, "comes down with the virus, you're going to need help. You're isolated at your farmhouse. Here, you have us to take care of you. I agree with Simone, you need to feel comfortable with your living conditions."

He added, "If one of us becomes ill, there's an empty hotel where the person can live, and the rest of us can quarantine. We can hire private nurses, and the hospital is close by. You know we want you to continue living next door, where you have us to support you."

"This virus has gotten all of us on edge," Simone added. "I agree with Charlie, if one of us gets ill, we have options for quarantining, and being very close to a top-rated hospital. Please reconsider staying in Westport," Simone pleaded.

"May I say something?" Irene nervously interjected. "I know I said that I'd go back with you to Charlottesville, but I'd really prefer to stay here with Simone and Charlie."

Virginia Smith was astonished by her housekeeper's change of heart. "I would not want to go back to Virginia without you, Irene," she stammered. Quickly changing her tone, she said with slight irritation, "But if you'd prefer to stay here, then I guess I will return by myself."

"Oh no," Irene immediately objected. "Please, don't be upset with me. I'd never leave you alone in that big house. Who would cook and clean for you? Who would drive you to the grocery store, to the doctor, to visit Judy and Harold? No, I'll go with you, if you want to leave," she added. Now it was Irene's turn to search her purse for a tissue. She, too, dabbed at her eyes, doing her best to stay stoic.

"Is there something else going on, Mrs. Smith, that you're not telling us?" Simone asked. "You mentioned other 'things' and I'm curious what you mean by that. I'm sure you miss your husband, but going back to Charlottesville isn't going to change the fact that he's gone." Simone quickly added, "No disrespect to Mr. Smith. I miss him as well."

Mrs. Smith and Irene exchanged glances. Simone knew something was amiss. It normally took Mrs. Smith a long time to make a decision, and returning to the hills of the countryside wasn't one she made quickly or lightly.

Finally, Virginia Smith cut the silence. "I promised not to say anything." She hesitated before continuing. "So, I can't."

Several scenarios ran through Simone's and Charlie's minds. "Mrs. Smith, are you not well?" Charlie asked.

"I'm fine." But she still remained mute.

Charlie looked at Irene for an answer, but she lowered her eyes.

"Are you in trouble? Do you need money?" While Charlie's abrupt question seemed forward, he was troubled by something nefarious that seemed to be going on.

"Mrs. Smith, what's wrong?" Simone demanded. "Has someone asked you for money? Identity thieves are notorious for tricking the elderly out of their savings, and ghosting dead people."

"You should tell them," Irene whispered.

"Mrs. Smith, please don't make us drag the information out of you," Charlie said, now even more concerned. "Tell us, what is it?"

"I promised Judy I wouldn't say anything," she began. "And she'll be angry if I tell you."

Dead air consumed the room as they braced themselves for Virginia Smith's response.

Finally, she spoke. "Judy and Harold are expecting a baby in November."

"Oh my God!" Simone shouted as she jumped from her seat and ran over to Mrs. Smith, throwing her arms around her, and expressing words of shock, joy and love.

"This is great cause for celebration," Charlie said, going over to the wine bar and removing a bottle of chilled Moet & Chandon champagne. Then he removed four flute crystal glasses from the mahogany wood cabinet.

"A toast to the happy couple, and future grandmother," he said, popping the cork. He carefully poured the bubbly into the glasses, and passed them around the table.

"Oh, this is delicious, Charlie," Irene said. "But I remember one Christmas dinner in Paris when you got me drunk. You're not doing *that* again," she giggled, before taking another sip.

"Why couldn't you tell us?" Simone asked.

"She's in the very early stages, Simone. Possibly only three weeks. She wants to be sure, and she wants to tell you herself. So please, my dear, promise me you'll act surprised when she does pass along the news.

"Of course, we will."

Charlie stood and raised his glass. "Here's to a new addition to the family: a child to grow alongside our children. To be cousins and friends for life, and who together will make this world a better place. Saluté."

"To all, good health and happiness," Simone said, as their glasses clicked in unison.

Twenty-Three

"Hi, Dr. Brady," Jennifer said when he returned her call. It's Jennifer Keys, the woman with the dog and the cane."

"I think I remember you," he said, jokingly. "To what do I owe the pleasure of this call? Are you missing me already?" he teased.

Jennifer wanted to yell, "Yes!" into the phone, but remained composed, though a tad breathless. "I hurt my ankle, again. I'm in Florida, and I was chasing Goober . . . he was rescuing a toddler from a crocodile. It was being shot at by the police . . . things thrown at it by the lifeguards . . . and people were screaming . . . I was running . . . and I fell on the wet, hard sand . . ."

"Whoa." Mike Brady said. "Slow down, please. You were chasing a crocodile?"

"No, Goober was. It's a long story, but I fell and hurt my ankle."

"If the airlines hadn't curtailed flights, I'd be on the next plane out to examine your ankle, and listen to the long story. Every word of it," he assured Jennifer.

Jennifer was taken aback. "Oh," was all that tumbled out of her mouth. *I'm such an idiot,* she thought to herself.

Further composing herself, she added, "I don't think it warrants you flying down here, but it's wonderful to know that you'd do that for me."

"Only for you," his voice grew deeper.

Jennifer's stomach flip-flopped.

"When are you coming back home? I'd like to see you. But I can't be your doctor any longer."

"I'm confused," she said.

"What's confusing, Jennifer? I like you, and I'd like to see you, but not as your physician. I can't date a patient. So, when are you returning to Connecticut?"

She tried sounding calm, but his words were an aphrodisiac.

"I'm working a wedding tomorrow morning. It's a very small gathering; only six people attending because of the virus. Goober and I have a flight back to Hartford, arriving at 8:30. That is, if the flight isn't canceled. The airline assured me this afternoon that they're flying until this weekend."

"I'll pick you up at the airport," Michael offered.

"Well," she hesitated. "It's not that simple. The bride and her dog will be with me. Besides, my car is at the airport. So, I won't need a lift. But thank you for the lovely gesture."

"The bride?" he asked. "Won't she be with her husband, going off on a honeymoon?"

"It's complicated," she said. "Another long story."

"Perhaps we can meet over the weekend, when you can tell me two very long stories?" he said flirtatiously.

"Dr. Brady . . ."

"Mike," he interrupted. "Please, call me Mike."

"Okay," Jennifer said, pausing for a moment to catch her breath. "Mike, I'm concerned about the virus. Several cases have been reported in Key Biscayne. I don't know how it is in Connecticut, but I'm so afraid of picking it up on the flight home, and infecting you. I plan on quarantining at home for two weeks before seeing Simone."

"How about we do FaceTime? Does that work for you?" he asked.

"That would be perfect." Her face felt flushed just like a teenager's, anxious about her first date.

"Is it swollen?" he asked.

"Is what swollen?"

"Your ankle, young lady," he said, laughing.

"Sorry. Yes. Yes, it is."

"Put ice packs on it every few hours for twenty minutes at a time. That should help. Take two aspirin, and call me in the morning."

"Seriously?" she asked. *I'm such a jerk*, Jennifer thought to herself.

"Yes, seriously. I look forward to hearing from you tomorrow. Until then, get some rest."

"I will, doctor. I mean, Mike."

Jennifer hung up, feeling like a goofy adolescent.

Twenty-Four

By Tuesday afternoon, both women were feeling the strain of the events of the past few days. It was only the day before that Goober had saved a child from the jaws of a crocodile, Jennifer had injured her ankle and the whole world was facing a pandemic. Things could not seem bleaker.

"Caroline, if you don't mind, I'm going to order room service tonight," Jennifer said. "My ankle is bothering me, and I can't walk outside my room without someone asking to take a selfie with Goober. Are you all right with that?"

"That's fine," Caroline said. "The JP called and asked to meet at five o'clock to go over details. I'll get a salad to go, and eat in my room afterwards. I also need to talk to my sister and confirm she's going to show up in the morning. I bet she's already checked out and is back home in New Jersey."

"I'd assume she would have told you she was going home," Jennifer said. "She sounds so inconsiderate, Caroline, but I don't think she'd go as far as to try to ruin your day."

"You don't know Wanda. She would stop at nothing. She's hated me since I was a child. She'd rip the heads off my dolls, or cut their hair, just to see me cry. She could be so vindictive and nasty. Seriously, she's probably back home."

"I'm sorry she's added such stress to your event."

Jennifer realized that the word 'wedding' stuck in her throat. She still couldn't assimilate Caroline marrying herself, but she was there to do a job, and she had to follow through. There were many times Simone and she had planned a wedding, and it was obvious, the couple didn't belong together. The same with Caroline: she wished to have a ceremony with which Jennifer may not agree, but she did not have any right to judge.

Caroline sat at one of the high-top tables by the pool. The waiter took her order. "I'd like seltzer with a dash of cranberry juice, two olives, and a twist of lime. Please serve it in a martini glass." He paused for a moment, nodded, and left. Soon, her faux cosmopolitan appeared before her.

Caroline wondered what the Justice of the Peace looked like. She tried to Google him, but nothing came up, other than a man by the same name who was a champion gamer. No photos were available; not on Facebook or any other social media venue.

At precisely five o'clock, a disheveled looking man, with wrinkled shorts and shirt approached her table. "Caroline?"

She looked up and faced a cherub of a man. He was short and chubby with a baby face. "Yes."

"Hi, I'm Reginald Brown. Reggie, for short." They shook hands.

The waiter approached. Reggie ordered a Stella beer. When the waiter left, Reggie adjusted himself in his chair before speaking. "So, you want to marry yourself," he said, stating the obvious.

Caroline found him to be nervous, uncomfortable, and socially awkward. "Yes, that's the plan."

"You know it's not legal in the United States," he said. "I mean, I can do the service, and all, but there's no legal documents to sign. I think you need to know this, in case you wondered." He continued rambling on nervously about the legal implications, but Caroline wasn't listening. She found herself staring at his mouth, which seemed inviting. His teeth were white and even, and his lips were plump, like the rest of his body. "So, why do you want to marry yourself?" he asked.

Caroline realized he had just asked her a question. "I'm sorry, what?"

"Why do you want to marry yourself?" he repeated.

"Because I'm fat," she blurted out. Immediately, she regretted admitting that, especially since she was sitting across from a man who was equally heavy. "I mean," she groped to find the appropriate words, "I've never had a boyfriend, and I don't think I'll ever get married. But I want a wedding."

"Are you having a reception afterwards?"

"No, I'm not. I'll have one after this virus is over."

"Will you come back to Florida to do the party? Will you do another service with your family in attendance?" The barrage of questions kept coming.

"I don't know," she answered. "You're starting to make me doubt this whole idea."

"I'm sorry, Caroline. I don't mean to confuse you. I'm trying to figure out what I'm supposed to say to you tomorrow during your service . . . if it's called a service."

"Have you ever done a sologamist wedding?"

"No."

"Oh," she said staring into her empty glass. She was starting to feel hungry. A Milky Way would satisfy her with instant gratification. She shook her head as to push the thoughts of candy out of her mind.

"Are you okay?" Reggie asked, noticing her mood changed suddenly. He signaled to the waiter for another round of drinks.

"I'm fine. It's just that so many things have gone wrong since I started this journey, that I'm wondering if I'm being realistic. My family isn't attending . . . I don't know if my sister will show up . . . everything is shutting down around me." Her words drifted off.

"I don't know why you think no one would want to marry you, Caroline. I think you're a very pretty woman."

Reggie's sentiments momentarily stunned her. She looked into his eyes. They were sparkling. *It's the booze talking*, she convinced herself. "Thank you," she murmured.

"Seriously, I think you're very pretty. You shouldn't give up on yourself. Look at me. No one wants to date a fat schlub like me. I'm a gamer. I live at home with my parents, play video games all day, and I don't date."

"How do you make a living?"

"I've obtained certificates online for a slew of occupations. I'm a web designer, paralegal, interior designer, and a minister. You can get dozens of certificates online, so I get them. I do fairly well creating web designs. What do you do for a living?" he asked.

"I'm an influencer for beauty products. People read my blogs and believe the products I'm promoting are the latest and greatest. I also am "the voice" for several authors on audio books. So, I understand how you – like I – hide behind our computer screens."

"We have a lot in common," Reggie said. "I'm feeling the effects of this beer. Want to grab a burger?"

Caroline envisioned eating a fat, juicy burger with sharp cheddar cheese melting down its sides, along with mouth-watering fries. It sounded wonderful, but she reminded herself how far she had come, and she refused to undo all her hard work by falling backwards. Although the road she was traveling seemed bumpy and challenging, she had to stay focused on her goals.

"I'd love to have something to eat, but I'd prefer a salad or fresh fish," she said rather sheepishly.

"I'm sure there's something on the menu you can find to eat." He motioned to the waiter again and asked for menus.

Caroline ordered a grilled grouper with lemon, and steamed vegetables. "No bun," she added.

"Do you want fries with that?" the waiter asked.

Oh, how Caroline craved hot salty fries. "No, thank you," she murmured.

Reggie ordered a medium-rare cheese burger with jalapenos, bacon, lettuce, tomato and sweet potato fries. "Have to have some veggies," he chuckled.

They chatted well into the evening. After dinner, Caroline drank herbal tea, while Reggie had another Stella – his third - and a scoop of chocolate ice cream. All through dinner, she craved what he was eating, but she was never tempted to ask for so much as a fry, or a taste of his ice cream. She felt strong, and comfortable talking to Reggie. He didn't judge or mock her. He said she was pretty. Those words stuck in her mind.

"When are you going back home?"

"Tomorrow, after the ceremony." She hesitated before speaking again. "Reggie, do you think I'm being silly wanting to marry myself?"

He paused for a moment. "Honestly, Caroline, I still don't understand why you think no one would marry you. You're smart, pretty, and a great conversationalist. Why have this ceremony if no one is coming or having a reception afterwards?"

"Do you think I should cancel?"

"I can't answer for you. You've come this far. I know you have your heart set. I'm happy to say a few "promising" words tomorrow morning. But, if you decide at the last minute to cancel, that's fine with me, too. If you decide to cancel, please let me know before I head out in the morning. There's nothing worse than a no-show bride."

"I'll let you know if anything changes. I've come to Key Biscayne to get married, and married I will be," she answered with determination.

He escorted her to the elevator, and wished her a good night's sleep. "I'll see you in the morning," he said as the doors closed.

Caroline found herself smiling. "He thinks I'm pretty," she said aloud as the elevator carried her up to her floor.

Twenty-Five

The following morning, Jennifer woke up at five o'clock. Sleep had not been a friendly visitor. She had tossed and turned all night obsessing about Mike, the wedding, the spread of the virus, and especially the flight home. Her biggest concern was the flight being canceled. How would she get back to Connecticut? She chided herself for allowing so many stressful thoughts to consume her. She finally decided she had to focus on the wedding, and put her anxieties aside. "SOAP!" she said aloud.

Her ankle felt sore, but better than yesterday. She took her cane, and left the room to walk Goober along the grassy area behind the hotel. A couple walking the path stopped and asked if this was the dog that had rescued the child.

"Yes, he is."

They praised her for having such a brave and smart dog. "Check today's newspaper," the husband shouted, as they continued their walk.

Jennifer feared the newspaper would be filled with horrors about the virus, or, worse, that all flights leaving Florida were canceled. She might have to rent a car – if one was available – and drive back to Connecticut. She anticipated long lines at gas stations, abandoned hotels along I-95, and spending two long days in a car.

She returned to the lobby, where she was stopped by the concierge. He handed her a copy of *The Islander News*, Key Biscayne's weekly paper. There, on the front cover, was a photo of Goober carrying the child by its diaper with the caption: *DOG RISKS LIFE TO SAVE TODDLER.* "Your dog is a rock star," he said as he petted Goober's head, and returned to his station.

Jennifer stared at the front page, not believing her eyes. "Wow" she mumbled. She looked up and saw hotel guests pointing at her. Before people asked for a paw-autograph, or a selfie with Goober, she quickly turned and took the elevator up to her room.

She began packing, anxious for the ceremony to be over, so she could get to the airport. If there was room on an earlier flight, they'd take it. Even if it meant going coach. She put on a simple sun dress with a sheer shawl and flats, paying extra attention to her hair and makeup. "This is as good as I'm gonna get," she said to Goober, who barked his approval. She checked out of her room remotely, using the hotel's TV service. She didn't want to walk through the lobby again, being stopped for a photo with Wonder-Dog-Goober.

Jennifer put her suitcase in the trunk, and headed down the path leading to the marsh. The photographer was there, setting up a tripod, and two light umbrellas. Jennifer checked her watch: 8:25. She wondered where Caroline, her sister and her family were. She realized that her nerves were getting the best of her. She just wanted to be on a plane, settled in her seat, heading back home. She realized then that the suggestion of going through with this ceremony was not a good idea after all. Instead, they should have left immediately, since every day the coronavirus numbers in Florida were escalating.

As these thoughts raced through her mind, Goober began to whine. "What is it, boy?" He looked up at her and barked. He barked again, a second, third and fourth time. She decided he was sensing her anxiety, and was trying to help calm her down.

Suddenly, Caroline and the Justice of the Peace, came walking down the path. They were chatting like old friends, occasionally laughing. He helped her take the final step from the walkway onto the grassy area.

Caroline wore a white tea length dress. A decorative comb adorned her hair, with an extraordinarily long flowing train attached. Low silk pumps completed the outfit. Adding to the festivities, Pyewacket wore a tiny red bow tie around his neck.

"You look lovely, Caroline," Jennifer said.

"Thank you. It's a dream come true. This is the best day of my life," she said, her face aglow. Jennifer noticed Caroline was wearing contacts instead of her heavy black framed eyeglasses. Her eyes sparkled and Jennifer felt guilty for wanting the ceremony to be over, so she and Goober could get home. Instead, she tried focusing on her job as Caroline's wedding planner. Successfully, she managed to put her selfish thoughts aside.

"Is your sister here?" Jennifer asked.

"She called me yesterday saying they had arrived. So much for my saying she went back to New Jersey. But she gave me grief about having to do this."

"She'll get over it," Jennifer assured her. "Today is *your* day, so don't let anyone spoil it for you."

"Here's the bad news," Caroline added. "They're on the same flight as we are. It was the only one they could get."

"But we'll be in first class."

"That's right!" Caroline said, smiling. "We won't see her, and she'll be so jealous we're not in coach with them."

Jennifer handed her bride a small bottle of water. "Take a few sips, so you'll be hydrated." She adjusted her veil so that it would flow all the way down to the grass.

Suddenly, from behind Caroline's back came the sound of her sister's voice, yelling at her daughter Stella for falling down while she skipped along the path. Caroline turned quickly around. Wanda was wearing a tank top, jean cut offs, and flip-flops. Her husband wore shorts and a tee shirt with the logo, "Visit Florida" including a large, pink flamingo emblazoned across his chest. Stella had on a bikini, bright magenta plastic sunglasses and tiny flip-flops.

Caroline stared at her sister. No words could express her hurt and embarrassment, and her deep and growing rage.

"OK, we're here," Wanda said, rolling her eyes. "Let's get on with it. We want to go to the pool before we have to check out."

"What the hell is wrong with you, Wanda?" Caroline shouted. "How could you come to my wedding dressed like you just walked off the beach?"

"You said I could wear anything I wanted, remember?"

Jennifer stepped in between the two women, to avoid what she envisioned could become an escalating situation. "Wanda," she said calmly. "I thought you'd realize your sister was having a wedding. Do you have any appropriate clothing you could change into?" Jennifer's words were calm, but firm.

"No, I don't. Everything's packed."

Caroline walked around Jennifer, and stood inches from her sister "You'd do anything to ruin my day," she yelled.

"If you don't like it, we can leave."

"Why don't you," Caroline said. She turned her back on Wanda, who was still screaming about the inconvenience of the event. Caroline headed down towards the marsh for photos. She picked up Pye, and tried her best to look happy.

Goober began barking again.

"Stop it," Jennifer said, annoyed at Wanda, the whole situation, and now her dog. But Goober continued to bark. She took his leash firmly in her hand, and headed down towards the water. She tied Goober's leash to a nearby bench, commanded him to sit and stay. Then she attended to her bride by fluffing her veil and checking Caroline's makeup.

"Do you want your sister and her family to join you?" the photographer asked.

"No," Caroline said. "I don't want her in any of my photos."

Wanda yelled back, "Well, I don't want to be in any of your photos. You fat cow."

The ugly scenario continued. Wanda quickly walked down to where Caroline stood at the edge of the marsh, with Pye in her arms. Goober began barking incessantly, Pye followed suit, and started wiggling in Caroline's arms. The two women continued screaming at each other.

Suddenly, Jennifer gave out a shriek. "Caroline, a croc!" she yelled over the two women's voices. The Justice of the Peace, who had his back to the marsh, and the photographer, quickly scurried away from the water.

Wanda, instead of pulling her sister away from the water's edge, gave her a push closer to the edge. A crocodile quickly and stealthily swam towards her.

Something pulled on Caroline's veil. She gave out a blood-curdling scream, resonating loudly above Goober's barking. Pye whimpered as Caroline squeezed her grip on him. The crocodile had a hold on Caroline's veil and began jerking her head backwards. His ravenous-looking mouth opened and shut as the length of the veil disappeared into his throat.

"Pye!" Caroline yelled frantically. The little dog, the likely target of the crocodile, cried as she squeezed him closer to her. Then quickly, without thinking, she tossed the little dog towards the grass. He was caught by the photographer. Everyone stood in horror as they watched Caroline's head being twisted left and right, while being dragged down by the crocodile.

Twenty-Six

During these unprecedented times, Simone spent most of her days researching creative wedding ideas. Several couples decided to elope within days of the upcoming shutdown. City halls were bombarded with requests for marriage licenses and justices of the peace. Ministers and other religious leaders were being called upon to perform emergency ceremonies. Families were disrupted by disagreements between couples and parents, and fears of the unknown ran rampant. Simone tried to play referee, but in most cases, she was unsuccessful.

Gatherings were strictly prohibited. There was nothing she could do to alter that reality. Every vendor Simone had employed, closed up their businesses. Some might never recover from the impact of the crashing economy.

"I Do" had seventeen weddings, six graduations, several Holy Communions, three Bar Mitzvahs, and six baby showers booked between April and July. It was their busiest time of the year, and the majority of their income. One by one, Simone had to call clients to tell them they would have to reschedule their event until the fall, or if the virus continued to be out of control, possibly as late as next year.

Disappointment took precedence as these notifications had to be done over the phone, rather than in person. It all seemed so impersonal, cold, and daunting, very much like the virus itself.

"I don't care what the governor said, I want my wedding," one bride demanded.

"I know you do," Simone said, "and one day it will happen. But for now, that's not possible. Would you consider waiting until the end of the year?"

"No," the woman said firmly. "Besides, by May this whole thing will blow over."

"Or not," Simone stood firm. "We need to be prepared. The scientists think the virus might take longer to eradicate than what is being reported."

"I want my wedding," the bride was annoyingly relentless, ignoring Simone's explanations.

"Please, consider this: the purpose of your wedding day is to marry the man you love. Correct?"

No response.

Simone pressed on. "Your wedding isn't just about one day. It is about a lifetime of being with that person."

The conversation went downhill from there. The bride insisted on having her wedding on June twentieth, refusing to listen to any of Simone's suggestions, no matter how much she tried reasoning with her.

"If we try to cancel the vendors now, three months before the wedding, you'll have a greater chance of getting reimbursed. I can't promise any refunds if you wait until May."

"I'll take my chances," the woman said.

"In that case, my company cannot take that risk. Therefore, I am releasing you from your contract. In the future, if your wedding is canceled, "I Do" will not negotiate refunds with the contracted vendors. You will be receiving a letter to that effect, stating the terms of termination."

"You're firing me as a client? Of all the nerve. I've never been so insulted in all my life," the future bride said indignantly. She continued with a litany of insults and curses.

Simone ignored her rant. Over the years, she had developed a thick skin to the insults by so-called entitled bridezillas. This one would not listen to reason, so Simone had to cut her loose.

"You'll be charged to date for the hours invested."

Fortunately, she had given Simone a substantial deposit, enough to cover the hours already put in. "I will send you a complete accounting within the next three weeks. I wish you all the best. Goodbye." Simone hung up, feeling disgusted and annoyed. She simply chalked it up as another 'occupational hazard.'

One call after another became tedious and frustrating. A few cancelations were accepted graciously, but not enough to make her job easier. Simone felt sad for these couples and families, who had planned and booked a year ahead, or more. But the forces of nature could not be stopped. This virus was deadly.

She noted the time; ten minutes to noon. Caroline's wedding reception, would have ended by now. She wondered why Jennifer hadn't texted her after the ceremony. She assumed Jennifer must be busy packing, and would soon be heading to the airport. She had mentioned wanting to book an earlier flight.

Simone put her cares behind her, and joined Charlie for lunch a few minutes later, along with their seven-month-old twins, now sitting in high chairs. Virginia Smith and Irene sat nearby, hovering over the babies. The twins had developed some dexterity with picking up food from a dish on their high chairs. Most of it, however, landed on the floor, in their hair and on their faces, which Simone, the proud mother, found amusing and endearing. Afterwards, they all played until it was time for the twins' afternoon naps.

Simone and Charlie went back to their respective desks to complete their work for the day. Simone returned couples' calls, whose dream weddings were now turning into nightmares. She worked hard to obtain returns of deposits from vendors, and especially the banquet halls. She realized what the Hamilton family was dealing with, being one of the largest and most expensive venues in Connecticut. They were possibly facing a major irreversible financial crisis. No one knew how long the shutdowns would last. Smaller boutique facilities suffered as well and might be forced to shut their doors forever. If a florist, caterer, banquet facility, or photographer went out of business for good, it would be nearly impossible to get deposits returned.

Simone fought fiercely for a one-hundred percent return for each couple. Some vendors didn't return her calls. Others were understanding and accommodating. Weddings that were booked for a future date had a better chance of having the full amounts returned. But the events booked in March or April, were more complicated. Agreed deposit returns ranged between twenty and thirty percent. Often, a manager explained they couldn't afford to return any of the deposit. It became a futile situation.

Simone had worked with many of the vendors before. She reminded them of past business, and assured them "when this is over, you'll be the first one on my call list." *If it ever will be over,* she mused. The workers' spirits were broken. They felt utterly dejected with no hope in sight. But Simone instinctively felt that she, and most likely her company, would survive. Others might not be as lucky. Many professionals would be forced to close, never to open their doors again. It was going to be a big financial hit to her income, but legally, and morally, she knew it was the correct thing to do.

When three-thirty came around and calls to Jennifer's phone continued to go to voice mail, Simone became concerned. She decided to call the hotel confirming that Jennifer and Caroline checked out.

"Oh, miss, there was a terrible accident this morning involving the wedding party." The manager proceeded to tell Simone about the catastrophe, the arrival of the police, EMS, and how several people were taken to the hospital.

Simone listened in shock to the manager's tale. Then, she immediately rushed to Charlie to report the news.

"The manager said the biggest danger is going to the hospital, and ending up contracting COVID. Charlie, I don't know what to do. I fear something terrible has happened to Jennifer."

"Did the manager say who was injured?"

"No, he didn't know. He was only informed by a staff member on duty this morning. He promised he would try to obtain additional information, and call me back. Unless I start calling all the hospitals in the Miami area, I may never find out what happened to Jennifer and Caroline."

Charlie embraced his wife. She pressed her face into his shoulder and began to cry.

"I'm sure she's okay, my love. I'm sure *they're* okay." But his words were not convincing.

Twenty-Seven

Caroline screamed for help as the crocodile thrashed her about. The reptile had her veil lodged in its mouth, continuing to drag her under the water.

Pye, no longer the crocodile's target, wiggled and barked, trying to pry himself loose from the photographer's grip. Stella began screaming, "Look, mommy! Just like Peter Pan." Her father grabbed his daughter, lifted her in his arms, and hurried back toward the beach club. Wanda stood and watched, puffing on a freshly lit cigarette, her addictive and reliable 'security blanket.' Jennifer held fast onto Goober's leash. The dog was frantic, barking and lunging toward the water. It took all of her strength to contain him.

Reggie turned to Jennifer and grabbed the cane out of her hand. "Sorry," he said. With that, he charged into the water to rescue Caroline.

It appeared the crocodile was choking on her veil, opening and closing its jaws. It took perfect timing, but when it opened his mouth again, Reggie jammed the cane inside and down its throat. Reggie quickly ripped the comb out of Caroline's hair, allowing the veil to continue filling the beast's mouth. Reggie pulled at Caroline until she was able to stand and run the short distance to land. Her dress was torn and caked with dirt. Her face was smeared with makeup, blood poured from several gashes on her head and down onto her white dress. Sirens filled the air, drowning out Jennifer's screams, and the photographer ordering the others to run back to the beach club. Wanda led the pack, hollering for help, as if she herself was the victim of the attack.

Caroline fell hard on her knees, dripping fresh blood. Meanwhile, the crocodile snapped Jennifer's cane in half. It swam backwards, releasing the veil from its throat, and then turned its attention toward the evil doers, who had kept it from its vulnerable prey: a sweet-smelling little dog.

Reggie scooped up Caroline in his arms like a limp rag doll. He wasn't a big man, but adrenaline soared through his muscles. He carried her several feet before placing her on the ground. The commotion of police, firemen and an ambulance frightened the crocodile enough to return to the muck of the marsh.

Goober pulled on his leash, causing Jennifer to fall. The dog stopped and barked as if to say 'sorry, but you need to run.' Her purse slid off her shoulder, the contents emptying onto the grass. A policeman rushed over and helped her stand up. He instructed her to wait by the ambulance, just as an additional EMS truck arrived, and stretchers were removed.

Caroline was attended to first, with Reggie constant-ly by her side. He held her hand, and asked if he could ride with her to the hospital. The medic nodded. Jennifer was tended to next, her ankle beginning to swell, and her knees were bleeding profusely. She begged for Goober to ride with her, pointing out the therapy tag around his neck.

"It's unusual," the emergency personnel said, "but okay." The dog jumped in the back of the vehicle, as Jennifer was gently lifted up and onto a stretcher.

The only one left behind was the photographer, who promised to bring Pye back to his house. "I have a dog, so I don't mind." Jennifer said she would get in touch once they were discharged from the hospital.

Meanwhile, Wanda and her family were nowhere to be found.

Jennifer sat in an ER wheelchair, after being examined and approved for discharge. Her ankle was wrapped with a bandage, and she had adhesive strips on both knees. Goober sat attentively next to the wheelchair.

Jennifer waited anxiously for news about Caroline's condition. She suddenly realized Goober hadn't been walked, or fed for hours. She rolled up to the nurse's station, announcing she was taking her dog outside, and that she'd be right back. The nurse, oblivious, didn't bother to lift her head. Jennifer asked the security guard for the time. "It's two-thirty, Miss." *Where had the time gone?* she wondered.

She needed to call Simone with an update, and request she contact the airlines. If they couldn't get a flight tonight, or if Caroline had to stay another day or two, where was she going to sleep? How would she get food for Goober? So many questions cluttered her mind. She reached for her purse to call Simone, but it was gone. She remembered that it had fallen, the contents left on the grass, including her phone.

She then returned to the nurse's station, "Excuse me, may I please use your phone?" she inquired politely.

"I'm sorry, but the phones are only for the medical staff. There's a pay phone in the cafeteria," the nurse said, without lifting her eyes.

"But I don't have any money, and I need to make phone calls."

"I'm sorry, but we can't give money to everyone who wanders in here," she said, turning up her nose at Jennifer as if she were a street urchin. "And, we don't allow dogs in the hospital. He'll have to be tied up to a pole outside."

"He's my therapy dog," Jennifer said, trying to convince the nurse she was a patient, and not a beggar. "If you won't give me money for a phone call, then could you do me a favor and call my physician in Connecticut?"

But the nurse simply continued typing, and didn't respond.

"He's Doctor Michael Brady, Chief of Orthopedics at Yale-New Haven Hospital. Please, can you call him for me?" Jennifer pleaded.

"I explained, we don't make phone calls for people," the nurse said rudely.

Jennifer's ire was mounting. She knew that the 'squeaky wheel got the grease,' so she raised her voice. "Help me," she yelled. "Can someone please help me?"

"What's going on here?" another nurse asked. "I'm Jovita Ladipo, the floor supervisor. What exactly is happening here?"

Jennifer jumped in: "I was injured trying to escape a crocodile attack. My client, a bride, was dragged into the water by the reptile. I've lost my purse, cell phone, money – everything. I'm trying to contact my associate to let her know that I'm safe. Or, my doctor in Connecticut. But I can't seem to get any cooperation," she said, giving the curt nurse a hard stare.

Nurse Lapido came around from the station. She looked at Jennifer's wristband, tapping the information into one of the laptops.

She turned to Jennifer. "Please, give me your attending doctor's name in Connecticut." Jennifer supplied Mike Brady's information, all the while tossing disparaging looks at *Nurse Ratchett*.

"Would you like something to drink or eat?" she asked, warmly.

Jennifer said she wasn't hungry, but her dog could use some water and food. "Thank you. You're very kind."

"You have to understand, we get several vagabonds in here daily, many looking for drug money, meds or alcohol. I assume the nurse didn't see your patient bracelet. I'm sorry."

She wheeled Jennifer over to the nurse's lounge, where she took a sandwich from the refrigerator, placed it on a paper plate, and deposited it on the floor in front of Goober. "I hope he likes meatloaf," she said.

"His favorite. Thank you. But you shouldn't have to give up your lunch for him."

"I don't mind. I need to lose a few pounds anyway," she joked.

She handed Jennifer an energy bar and a bottle of water. She poured water into a bowl for Goober. He wolfed it all down in minutes. Then, she removed her cell phone from her pocket, and searched the web for Dr. Michael Brady. Soon she was talking to him, and explaining what had happened to his patient. She listened intently "I see," she said, looking over at Jennifer and smiling. "She's safe here, doctor. We'll take good care of her, don't worry. And yes, her dog is with her, too."

Nurse Ladipo handed the phone to Jennifer. "Dr. Brady would like to speak with you." She turned and went over to the vending machine on the other side of the room, giving Jennifer the privacy, she assumed she wanted.

"Hello," Jennifer said, tentatively.

"Are you okay?" Michael Brady asked, sounding concerned.

"Yes, I'm fine. I don't know about Caroline, though. A crocodile grabbed her veil. And doctor," she lowered her voice and whispered, "Mike, her sister pushed her into the water, even though there was a croc nearby. It was awful. I really thought she was going to die."

"Now, you'll have three long stories to tell me," he said after being assured she wasn't seriously injured.

They chatted for a few more minutes, before Jennifer interrupted, "Would you mind doing me a favor? Please call Simone and tell her to call the airlines. Unfortunately, I don't know how long they're keeping Caroline here, so I can't say when we will be leaving Florida. Thank you. I am most appreciative for all your help, Mike."

"I'm happy to oblige," he said. "It's the least I can do. Please call me when you get back so I know you've arrived in one piece."

Jennifer handed the phone back to Nurse Ladipo and thanked her for her compassion. Goober looked up and let out a little conciliatory bark. "Let's find out what's going on with your bride," she said, as she pushed Jennifer's wheelchair back to the main lobby. She checked the charts, reporting that Caroline was taken for an MRI and CT scan. She was in room 302. "Take the elevator up to the third floor, and turn right."

"May I ask you a question?" Jennifer paused. "What about the coronavirus? Aren't you worried about it?"

"We've seen four cases at this hospital," she said, "but we know other hospitals in the area are starting to see an increase in numbers. I fear this is just the early stages. We've been lucky so far."

"Thank you, Nurse Ladipo. Be safe."

Jennifer found Caroline sitting up. Reggie was in a chair next to the bed, holding her hand, engrossed in a hushed conversation. They looked like a devoted couple, who had just survived a stunning life-altering experience.

Jennifer cleared her throat announcing her arrival. She pushed her wheelchair into the room asking, "Are you okay, Caroline?"

"I'm banged up, but I'm fine. Thanks to Reggie," she said, smiling at him. "He saved my life."

Reggie kissed Caroline's hand, and a huge smile crossed her face. Her entire demeanor had softened in just a few days.

Jennifer felt immense happiness for her client. *Maybe she has found love, after all,* she thought.

"The doctor said I can be released today," Caroline said, "and he gave me the all-clear to fly home tonight. Reggie will drive us to the photographer's house to get Pye before heading to the airport."

"That's wonderful news," Jennifer said. "But before we pick up your dog, I need to go back and get my purse. I hope it's still there. My identification, our airline tickets, and my cell phone were in it."

"Of course, Caroline said. "There's something I need to find, as well."

The three climbed into a cab and headed back to the *Key Biscayne Beach Club*. The two women, with the help of Reggie, limped down the path, and returned to where the morning's horrors had taken place. Fortunately, Jennifer's purse miraculously had not been moved. It was still lying in the same spot on the grassy area, its contacts scattered about. Reggie picked them up and placed them inside her purse.

Caroline looked around as if she, too, had lost something. She stopped suddenly, when she finally found it. "Jennifer, any chance you would possibly have a plastic bag?"

"Actually, I do," she said. I always keep several bags on hand to clean up after Goober." She handed one to

Caroline, who used it to store a cigarette butt, stained with bright pink lipstick.

"Let's get out of here," Caroline announced. "Reggie and I are going to pick up Pye. We'll meet you at the airport."

She and Reggie climbed into his car and headed to the photographer's house to pick up her dog. Jennifer got into her rental and drove to the airport, where she returned the car, and shuttle over to the main terminal.

"Your tickets were canceled, Ms. Keys," the check-in attendant said.

Jennifer had completely forgotten she had asked Simone to cancel them. "Oh, no. Are there any other seats available?"

The attendant tapped the keys on her computer and announced, "I do have seats in Business Class. I see you're traveling with two support animals. That's fine. Where is the other passenger?"

Jennifer pointed to Caroline, still wearing her wedding dress caked with mud and dirt. Pye was asleep on her lap.

The woman noted Caroline's torn and muddy wedding dress, and the bandages lining her head and arms. "My, she and the groom had a tough beginning. I hope they at least got married before she was injured."

"You can't begin to imagine. It's a long story. When can we board?" Jennifer asked, changing the subject.

"You can board in an hour. In the meantime, please have a seat, and relax."

Caroline and Reggie were deep in conversation, with kisses intermittingly exchanged. Jennifer felt like a voyeur. When the boarding call was finally announced, Jennifer, Caroline and the two dogs headed toward security.

"Caroline, please call me when you get home," Reggie said.

"I will," she promised, as she and Reggie hugged.

He watched as they passed through the scanners and into the other side, Reggie shouting, "I'll see you in two weeks," and blew a final kiss to Caroline.

She turned and reciprocated.

"What's *that* about?" Jennifer asked, slightly puzzled.

"Reggie is coming to visit me," she said, sounding almost giddy. "He's going to perform my food funeral, and join OA with Aunt Adele, too. I can't wait for her to meet him."

Jennifer didn't think it was her place to further interrogate Caroline, but she wondered if Reggie was eventually going to move in with her. Although the two had just met, stranger things have happened.

Twenty-Eight

The women and their animals arrived in Hartford, Connecticut. They had slept during the flight home, including the two dogs. Jennifer's car was at the airport, and Caroline's was at Jennifer's cottage in Milford. They drove to Jennifer's house, and she insisted that Caroline spend the night. "There's no need to rush back. And I have plenty of dog food."

Caroline agreed to stay, thanking Jennifer profusely. While driving back from the airport, they had ordered delivery from the local Italian restaurant. It was waiting for them on the front doorstep when they pulled into the driveway.

"I haven't had pizza in months. This is a real splurge," Caroline said, taking a bite of the still-hot cheesy slice. "Yum. I had forgotten how satisfying this could be."

Included was a large Italian salad of cherry tomatoes, torn romaine and radicchio leaves, black olives, and giardiniera pickled vegetables. A large container of Italian dressing was separate. Included was an order of sautéed broccoli rabe with garlic, which Caroline had never eaten before. She became an instant fan.

"Before I go to sleep, I'll call Aunt Adele," Caroline said. "I know it's late, but she must be worried. And I promised to call Reggie, too. Isn't he a dream?" she asked.

Jennifer nodded, not knowing if he was a nice guy or not. "He's certainly attentive," she said.

"Do you like leftover pizza, Jennifer?" Caroline asked, as she eyed the three remaining pieces in the pizza box.

"Not usually. Sometimes I put it in the freezer, or toss it. I try not eat too many carbs. But I can save it for you."

"I'd like to ask that you throw it out." Caroline announced stoically.

"Sure," Jennifer said, lifting the lid of the garbage can, and tossing the pizza inside.

"Do you have any abrasive cleanser?" Caroline asked.

Jennifer opened the cabinet under the sink, pulled out a container of Comet and handed it to Caroline. The woman sprinkled it liberally over the pizza staring up at her in the can. "I know this looks silly, but I've been known for taking left-overs out of the garbage and eating them in the middle of the night," she admitted. "But now, that's a thing of the past."

Jennifer shut the kitchen lights, and escorted Caroline upstairs to the guest room. "Sleep well," she said quietly closing the bedroom door. She returned to her bedroom suite on the first floor, still amazed by the Comet moment. *I guess she knows the devil within*, she thought.

She grabbed her cell phone and texted Mike that she was home, and they'd talk in the morning.

Twenty-Nine

Jennifer sent Simone a text at 11:15 p.m. She decided that the nanosecond ding was less jarring than a blaring phone. Simone immediately called her.

"I've been waiting to hear from you," she said. "Were you injured?"

"I'm fine," Jennifer reported. "My ankle is swollen, but I wasn't seriously hurt. Caroline, who is staying here tonight, is the one who received gashes on her head and arms. All her hospital tests were negative. It was very frightening to see the crocodile grab hold of her veil."

"How did she break loose?" Simone asked. "I thought once a crocodile attacked, it was impossible to disengage from its grip.

"Reggie, the Justice of the Peace, saved her life. He went in the water after her. He took my cane, and shoved it in the reptile's mouth."

"Oh, my. He sounds courageous."

"There's more. He and Caroline are an item," Jennifer continued, lowering her voice so that her house guest wouldn't overhear her. "They were kissing at the airport, and he's coming up to her house in a couple of weeks. I think she's in love."

"That's amazing," Simone said. "So, she never went through with the ceremony? Who knows . . . maybe she'll have a real wedding after all?"

"She's very happy, Simone. She's like a different person. Oh, and I'm leaving out the most important part. Caroline's sister Wanda, pushed her into the water."

"I don't believe that. Her own sister? The one she told us was so abusive?"

"That's the one. She showed up wearing cut-offs, a tank top and flip-flops. And when Caroline was screaming for help, Wanda took off in the opposite direction."

"You can't make this stuff up," Simone said.

"And here's another tidbit," Jennifer added. "When the three of us went back to the scene of the attack to retrieve my pocketbook, Caroline picked up a cigarette butt and put it in a baggie. I'm wondering why she'd do that."

"The only thing I can think of is DNA testing," Simone suggested. "But, why would Caroline want to do a DNA test on her own sister?"

"I don't know, and honestly, I'm too tired to figure it out. Good night, Simone. I'll call you tomorrow. You can update me on the latest and greatest things the twins are doing. Give them a kiss-kiss from Auntie Jenn."

"I will." Simone said good night and hung up. A DNA test, she wondered, as she climbed back into bed and snuggled up against her husband.

The next morning, Caroline arrived in the kitchen looking refreshed. "I slept very well. I'm a little sore, but considering the alternative, I'm doing okay."

"Glad to hear it," Jennifer said. How about a walk on the beach with the dogs before breakfast? I have an extra jacket hanging on the peg. Don't worry, there aren't any crocodiles in Milford. We've had whales breach a couple of times near Charles Island, but no pre-historic reptiles."

Jennifer grabbed a wooden walking stick, adorned with a carved ram's head, from the umbrella stand, and opened the back door. Goober charged down the steps, followed by Pye, whose little legs could only hop down one step at a time. Once on the sand, the poodle tried keeping up with his new BFF.

"Do you believe in love at first sight?" Caroline asked Jennifer as they walked along on the shore.

Jennifer considered her thoughts carefully before speaking. "For some, infatuation can be mistaken for love." She said nothing more, wanting Caroline to absorb her words.

They walked on in silence. The cold March wind was stinging Jennifer's face. They watched the two canines frolicking about, chasing seagulls and geese. Finally, finding the blustery weather too harsh, she whistled for Goober. He ran back, the poodle following closely behind. At the back door, the dogs got toweled off, and welcomed the warmth inside.

Jennifer began preparing breakfast for the dogs. Goober sat obediently, staring up at his mistress. He butt-dragged closer and closer to her, a routine he did every morning. Pye whined as he, too, watched Jennifer preparing food. Finally, the two bowls were placed next to each other on the floor, and being true to their nature, Goober and Pye ravenously scarfed down their breakfast with canine lust.

Meanwhile, Caroline set the table, and started a carafe of coffee. Jennifer cooked up eggs, whole grain toast, and put out two bananas. While they ate, the women chatted about the events that had taken place over the past few days, which now seemed more like months ago. Jennifer looked over at Goober, making sure he didn't bully the little dog by pushing him aside, so he could enjoy his food, too.

By ten o'clock, Caroline was back on the road with Pye curled up in the back seat, napping. She hummed as she drove the hour back to her Nyack apartment. She couldn't wait for Reggie's visit. But suddenly, a jolt of reality hit her: what if he wanted to have sex? She had never been with a man before. Who could she talk to about this? Certainly not her mother. Nor Aunt Adele, because she had never been married. There was talk of the man who broke her heart, but knowing Aunt Adele, she would never have had pre-marital sex. Not back in her day when such indiscretions were frowned upon. Caroline would have to give this some thought, but first, she had another project to research.

Back at her apartment, she settled down at her computer and began working. On her desk sat the lipstick covered cigarette butt, still inside the plastic bag. It took several hours, and a dozen phone calls, but she finally connected with a lab in New York State who agreed to do a DNA test. They had warned her the sample might be contaminated, thus not giving her accurate results. But she decided to persevere. She mailed the package overnight.

She would have to wait the six weeks before receiving results.

Then, she paid for a DNA kit from Ancestry.com, just in case the cigarette didn't yield any results. She wanted more information about her family's background, as her mother always dismissed her questions. The kit arrived in a few days, and she immediately mailed the tube back with her saliva. She would have to wait several more weeks for that. But during a pandemic, she had all the time in the world.

She called her Aunt Adele and updated her on the crocodile fiasco, Reggie, and Wanda's inappropriate attire, and how her sister had behaved. She gushed over Reggie, proclaiming she was in love. "He's so wonderful, Aunt Adele. He saved my life."

The two talked about his upcoming visit in early April. He would have to quarantine for two weeks, but afterwards, she wanted her aunt to meet him.

"Will he be staying in a hotel?"

"No, he'll stay with me." Caroline said. She suddenly added, "I have an air mattress."

"Caroline, you know I'd never tell you what to do, but be careful. Please, you must use protection."

"Aunt Adele," Caroline said, feeling embarrassed, her cheeks burning. "I feel awkward discussing this with you." Caroline desperately wanted to end the conversation. Instead, she began stammering, unable to find the appropriate words.

"Caroline, calm down," her aunt said. "I'm just giving you some unsolicited advice. Men . . . well, they sometimes want more than what a woman is willing to provide. And when they get it, they forget all about their conquest."

"Conquest?" Caroline said. "Is that what you think having sex with someone is all about?"

"Caroline," Adele said, "that's not what I meant. All I'm trying to suggest is that you should be careful."

There was silence on Caroline's end. Was it true that Aunt Adele had experienced something like this? No, she convinced herself, that was impossible.

"I have to go now. I have a pot of soup on the stove," Caroline lied. "Love you. Talk soon." And she hung up.

She then called her mother and told her about the aborted wedding. She reiterated the story of how Wanda had dressed for the occasion, and how she had pushed her into the water, almost getting her killed by a crocodile.

"You must have said something, that angered her. I do not believe your sister would deliberately put you in harm's way."

Caroline knew that her mother believed Wanda could do no wrong. She was the perfect child, who adhered to society's expectations: marriage, child, home, each in that order. Conversely, Caroline was the oddball, who followed a different drummer, not consistent with the mores of politically correct demands. She told her mother about Reggie, and that he was coming for a visit. When her mother began lecturing her on the dangers of having a stranger in her apartment, Caroline lied to her as well, feigning soup was on the stove. She quickly said goodbye and hung up.

The weeks dragged on. The coronavirus was reaching exorbitant new numbers. State after state were experiencing clusters of outbreaks, followed by shutdowns. The death toll was mounting, and there seemed nothing could stop the spread of this dreaded disease. Companies were going out of business, shutting their doors for good. In some communities, food lines stretched for miles. Hospitals scrambled – begging for personal protective equipment and ventilators. The outlook was depressing.

Meanwhile, Caroline's work as an influencer dried up. Overnight, people were not going to nail or beauty salons. She tried publicizing over-the-counter products, but within two weeks that also failed. Fortunately, her audio-book and podcast reading contracts began skyrocketing. Her employer shipped sophisticated equipment to her apartment. She found herself working ten to twelve-hour days, making her throat feel sore and her voice sounding raspy. When Reggie called at the end of each day, she could hardly speak.

Unfortunately, because of the high volume of cases of the virus in New York City and surrounding areas, a 'shelter-in-place' order was enforced until the end of April. Her rendezvous with Reggie would now have to wait until mid-May, or June. Meanwhile, they "saw" each other on Skype and FaceTime.

One night, Reggie called, saying most of the airlines had ceased flying, and it was difficult getting a flight out of Florida. He could drive, but it seemed many hotels were closed as well. "Can we wait another month? Maybe by May things will be better."

"I'm disappointed, of course," Caroline said, "though we have no choice but to wait." They continued their virtual conversations, and as the weeks drifted slowly by, Caroline noticed Reggie's face seemed thinner. "You're looking more svelte every day," she told him.

"I'm trying, but it's very difficult. I found an OA group online, that does Zoom meetings, but it's not the same as seeing and talking directly to other overeaters. It's not surprising how many people turn to food for comfort, especially during this pandemic. I find myself looking for salty foods, like chips and pretzels to satisfy my edible longings."

"You have to be strong, Reggie. You'll get through it," Caroline assured him.

Most of their online conversations were spent sharing recipes, and supporting each other through their mutual obsessive "food needs." Reggie said he had lost twenty pounds in three weeks. Knowing that men lose weight faster than women, Caroline congratulated him, not crushing his success by pointing out the differential between the sexes when dieting.

Then, unable to contain herself, she suddenly blurted out what Adele had said. "My aunt told me to be careful when you come to visit." Caroline hoped this would open the door to an honest discussion about his expectations. After all, they had been virtually dating for weeks.

"Oh?" There was silence on the other end of the phone.

"Reggie, did I upset you?"

"No. It's just . . . I mean, Caroline, I don't know how to say this, but I'm very shy when it comes to discussing sex. Can we just hold off and talk about it when I get there?"

"Of course," she said, catching herself while a tinge of uncertainty soared through her. *Could he be a virgin, too?* She didn't bring up the subject again.

Thirty

April 2020

Mid-April arrived, and so did Easter, spring, and a feeling of rebirth. Traditionally, Simone held an Easter egg hunt for the neighborhood children, hiding coins, candy or toys inside plastic, colorful eggs. This year, however, there weren't any eggs, baskets, or Easter outfits. Nor were there any family gatherings on Easter or on Passover. This was the season for First Holy Communions, proms, and graduations. Most events, if not all, were canceled, erasing photographic memories that would never come to be.

Seven months prior, Simone dreamed about how her twins would look in their adorable outfits, celebrating their first Easter. She wasn't going to allow the pandemic to spoil her children's holiday. She would purchase new outfits for them, hide plastic eggs around the house, and take an abundance of photographs. She refused to follow the news reports of *The Easter That Wasn't*.

Earlier that week, Simone learned that her Aunt Louise, who lived in her home state of Kentucky, had passed away from COVID-19. No one was allowed to visit her in the hospital, nor was there a formal funeral. She was cremated, and her remains were being held by a neighbor for a future memorial service. Simone wondered when that 'future' would be; two months, six months, or a year away?

Jennifer also learned that her alcoholic brother Terrence was on a ventilator in a Long Island hospital. He didn't heed the warnings, refused to believe the coronavirus wasn't more than a flu, and continued to socialize after work with his construction co-workers. Two of his buddies were also hospitalized as a result of COVID.

"It doesn't look good for your brother," Mrs. Bridgette Keogh told her daughter. "The doctor wants to check me too, as I have a slight fever, and nothing tastes right to me."

"Do you want me to come home?" Jennifer asked.

"No, no, stay away, my dear. Whatever this is, it will soon vanish. I'm sure I'm just run down."

"Take care of yourself, mother. I love you."

"I love you, too."

Those were the last words uttered between them. Bridgette was hospitalized the next day, and died seventy-two hours later.

The phone rang, and a voice inquired, "May I speak with Jennifer Keogh?"

"This is Jennifer Keys. My family's name is Keogh."

"This is Doctor Phillips from Long Island Hospital. I'm sorry to inform you that your mother, Bridgette Keogh passed away this morning from complications of COVID. I'm terribly sorry," he repeated.

"Oh no," Jennifer cried. "She had said she wasn't feeling well . . . but I never thought . . . what about my brother, Terrance," she added. "Is he okay?"

"Let me check," he said.

It seemed an eternity before the doctor returned. "Ms. Keogh." He quickly corrected himself. "I mean, Ms. Keys. I checked your brother's chart, and it appears he passed away two days ago, also from COVID. He had your mother as next of kin. I'm very sorry to have to report such devastating news." He informed Jennifer that the hospital was off limits to visitors. Her mother and brother would be cremated; their remains to be kept at the local funeral home.

Jennifer thanked the doctor, and hung up. Her hands were shaking as she disconnected from the call and hit the 'end' button on her cell phone. Her father, notorious for being the town drunk and the reason she changed her last name, had passed several years ago from cirrhosis of the liver. Now that her mother and brother had also died, she'd never felt so completely alone in her entire life.

She texted Simone and informed her of the news. "Please don't call or text me. I need some time alone, to gather my thoughts." She sent the same text to Mike Brady. But he didn't heed her request. Immediately, he called her and asked if she'd like to FaceTime. She readily agreed.

"Mike, I'm all alone. I have no one in my life."

"You have me," he said softly. "I wish I could be with you, to hold you in my arms."

They spoke for twenty minutes. Most of the time Mike listened to Jennifer crying about how her only living relatives were in Ireland. She had no one to spend the holidays with . . . no family . . . no relatives . . . she was an orphan.

Mike listened patiently as the reality of losing relatives settled in for Jennifer. Over the years he had comforted many who had lost family members, sometimes multiple people simultaneously. He recalled one family who had lost their six children in a house fire. The parents went food shopping, leaving the eldest in charge of his siblings. The sixteen-year-old attempted to make French fries. When the wet potatoes hit the hot oil, there was an explosion of fire. The kitchen drapes quickly caught fire, traveling up the walls to the bedrooms above, where four children were asleep. A young child of twelve was found in the bathtub. The burned body of the teenage boy was discovered on the front lawn.

Suddenly, Mike's pager went off, requiring him to return to the emergency room. 'I'm sorry, Jennifer. I have to go. It's all hands on deck," he said. "I'll call you later this evening. I'm sorry I can't be with you," he said sympathetically. "I know what a difficult time this is for you. But this virus . . . I've never experienced such grief and loss." His words trailed off, realizing Jennifer was now enduring the same agonies as many others.

The days dragged into a week. Jennifer kept herself busy with paperwork, the unfortunate task of calling Social Security, and informing her mother's church friends. The president of the Rosary Society said the ladies would prepare meals, and leave them on the doorstep. Jennifer explained that no one was living in the house, as her brother had also died, and she lived in Connecticut.

A week later, Jennifer received a call from the Long Island funeral home, informing her that the remains of her mother and brother were ready to be collected. "I'll be there tomorrow," she told the funeral director.

The drive to Long Island was often long and tedious with much traffic. Sometimes it took over two hours to reach her mother's home. But today, she was at the funeral home in thirty-five minutes. Since the pandemic, people had nowhere to go, so the roads were empty. She felt as if she was in a horror movie, where at any moment a huge ferocious monster would slam into her windshield.

Jennifer slipped on her mask. The similarly masked man in the dark suit greeted her at the door. His voice was somber and stilted, the grief reflected in his eyes. He presented her with two black boxes containing the family remains. There was also a small black velvet bag taped to her mother's box.

"What's this?" Jennifer asked opening the bag.

"It's what your mother wore when she was admitted to the hospital," he said in a low voice.

Suddenly, out of the pouch, fell her mother's Claddagh wedding ring. Jennifer picked it up and admired the intricate details. Two hands, representing friendship held a heart, signifying her parent's mutual love. Adorning the heart was a crown, for loyalty. Her parents had matching rings, and as long as Jennifer could remember, they were never removed from their hands. She assumed, that since her father was buried and not cremated, the ring was still in place on his finger for all eternity.

Jennifer returned to her cottage, and placed the two boxes inside her bedroom closet. She had no idea what to do with their remains, or with her mother's house she would now inherit. She knew Mike would know what to do.

Thirty One

May 2020

It was ten-thirty p.m. Caroline had just gotten out of the shower and was blow drying her hair when she heard her cell phone ring. *Who could be calling at this hour?* Fearing something had happened to her parents, she ran to answer it.

"Caroline, it's Reggie. I hope I'm not calling too late."

Her excitement was palpable. Trying to keep her enthusiasm under control, she replied, "Oh, Reggie. It's so good hearing from you. How are you feeling? I hadn't heard from you in three weeks, I was afraid you were upset with me."

"I got COVID, Caroline, which put me in the hospital for a week. Fortunately, I had a mild case."

"Oh no, I'm sorry to hear that. Reggie, are you okay?"

"Yes, I'm fine. Caroline, I'm really missing you. I want to see you. Would it be all right if I came up to New York?"

"Of course," she immediately replied. "But are you healthy enough to travel?"

"I am. I got clearance from my doctors. And I have antibodies to the virus, so the doctor thinks I'm not a carrier. My cousin is going to New York City on business, so we'll fly together. He's heading to New York next week. Is that too soon?"

"No, not too soon at all. I'll send you my address. Text me when you land. I can pick you up at the airport. But Reggie, will you have to quarantine for two weeks?" she asked, concerned about her own health.

"I've been home for over two weeks. How about you? Have you been out and about?"

"No, not at all. I haven't seen anyone in a long time, except on Zoom."

"Then, we should be fine," he assured her. "I can't wait to see you."

They made arrangements for Caroline to meet them at Westchester County Airport. The plan was for Reggie's cousin to rent a car, and go on to his own destination. Caroline would bring Reggie back to her apartment, though she had no idea how long he planned to stay. The old unsettled feelings began to surface as to where he was going to sleep. She did have an extra bedroom and an air mattress; she'd see how things developed.

The plane was on time with Reggie and his cousin arriving at one-thirty. He introduced her to his cousin, who seemed more interested in getting on his way, than meeting Caroline. She wondered what he thought of her, allowing Reggie, practically a stranger, to stay at her place. But she decided she could no longer worry about other people's attitudes. She was happy, and that was all that mattered.

They drove the twenty minutes to her apartment. "I love your avant-garde style, Caroline," he said as he took in her décor. "Really nice."

They transported his luggage into the guest room. "I hope you're okay with an air mattress," she said sheepishly.

"That's fine," he said shyly. "In fact, I was afraid to ask where I would be sleeping. I didn't want to seem presumptuous by assuming anything . . . we hardly know each other . . ." he stammered on. "I'm relieved you made the decision for us."

Caroline cooked dinner for them: baked salmon in lemon and Dijon mustard sauce, steamed broccoli, and a large tossed salad. "I hope you don't mind my diet food, Reggie."

"Now that you've mentioned it, Caroline . . ."

Oh no, here it comes, she thought. *He thinks I'm still fat.*

"I know women are sensitive about their weight, and I didn't know how to say it, other than, you look fabulous," he said. "Really great. Sexy, in fact."

"Oh stop," Caroline said, blushing. Then she coyly added, "Do you *really* think I'm sexy?"

Reggie laughed at her naivety. "I think you're a very sexy woman." He got up from his chair, walked over to her and gave her a passionate kiss. *"Very sexy,"* he whispered. The kiss turned into more kisses, deep with hunger and desire. Feelings stirred inside Caroline that she had never known before.

"I think we need to slow down, Reggie."

He withdrew his lips from hers. "I'm sorry. I didn't mean to be so forward. I just couldn't resist kissing you."

No one – ever – had uttered those words to her. She was overwhelmed, both by her desires, and the comfort level she felt. Still, they ended up sleeping in separate rooms.

The next morning, Caroline rose before he did. She made a pot of coffee, and an omelet filled with various vegetables was cooking in the oven.

"Good morning," Reggie said, as he kissed Caroline's neck. "Did you sleep well?"

She turned to his scruffy face. He needed a shave and his hair was disheveled from sleep. He wore a tee shirt with the name of a rock band across the front, and blue-plaid cotton pajama bottoms. He looked manly, and new desires began to surface inside her. "Good morning," she muttered. "Coffee?" He nodded.

Reggie showered while she finished preparing breakfast. They devoured the omelet, toast and finished off two carafes of coffee.

"It's such a nice day," she said. "Are you up for a walk along the waterfront? I'd like to show you Nyack. And later, have you meet my Aunt Adele over lunch."

"Sounds great. God, Caroline. I've missed you so much."

"I missed you, too," she said, planting a tender kiss on his cheek.

At one o'clock they met Adele at the Main Street Bistro.

"Wow," he said when the two met. "I can see the resemblance."

Adele quickly changed the subject, suggesting they get a table because the place filled up quickly.

Reggie, craving a juicy hamburger, ordered their specialty of the house: Angus beef with chipotle sauce, jalapenos, cheddar cheese, avocado slices with lettuce and tomato, and a side of fried onion rings. The burger was four inches high; he could barely fit it into his mouth. Caroline and Adele ordered a chef's salad with the dressing on the side.

"Caroline tells me you're from the Miami area," Adele said. "Have you lived there long?"

"My whole life," Reggie said. "My father is a contractor in Miami, and my mother is an accountant."

A contractor, Adele heard. *Could his father possibly be Marcelo? That's impossible,* she decided. *Miami is a large city; what are the odds of that?*

They casually chatted over cups of coffee. Reggie had a piece of cheese cake, but the women passed on dessert.

"How long are you staying in town?" Adele asked Reggie.

"As long as Caroline will have me," he said, reaching across and squeezing her hand.

"Oh, I see," she said with a judgmental tone, laced with disapproval.

"Aunt Adele," Caroline interjected. "Reggie is staying on an air mattress in my guest room."

"It's none of my business," she said curtly.

Suddenly, Adele announced she had work to do in her garden. "It was lovely meeting you Reggie." She put on her face mask, and quickly left, walking back to her car.

Caroline and Reggie remained at the outdoor café, and enjoyed people watching. "I think your aunt doesn't approve of me staying at your apartment," Reggie said.

"I agree. She has old-fashioned ideas. But I'm surprised she left so abruptly. I thought she'd be more open-minded, but I guess I was wrong. She never married, and I don't think she's ever had sex."

When the two returned to Caroline's apartment, she sent her aunt a text asking if she was upset with them. Adele answered she was not upset, just a lot to take in all at once. She realized she was rude for leaving so suddenly, but she was getting a headache. *He seems to be a very nice man*, she wrote.

He is, Caroline texted back. *Aunt Adele, I think I'm in love.*

But no text was returned.

Thirty Two

Caroline and Reggie spent their days touring the town of Nyack. They did a day trip to the Palisades, where they hiked the rocky terrain. Many restaurants were still closed, so they packed picnic lunches, which also helped Caroline keep with her diet. The subject of sex did not come up again, as they fell into a more relaxed routine for now.

"Reggie, I'm wondering if you would perform another ceremony."

"Are you going to try to marry yourself again?" he asked, with a twinkle in his eye.

"No. Obviously, that idea didn't work out very well," she said. Looking out over the hilltop to the river below, she chose her words carefully. "I'd like to have a funeral."

"Are you planning to knock someone off?" he joked.

She chuckled in return. "No. It's a food funeral. I want to bury all the bad foods that constantly tempt me . . . candy bars, fast food, desserts. I need to make them seem 'dead to me' and burying them will do exactly that. Would you perform the ceremony? I know my aunt wants to participate, as we've discussed this before. I just never thought of having an actual service, with an officiant."

Reggie was silent for a long time before he spoke. "Caroline, first, I need to apologize to you and your aunt. I ate like a pig at lunch . . . a cheese burger, onion rings, dessert, and a beer. I should have been more sensitive to you ladies. It must have been difficult watching me consume foods you two have avoided. I lost a lot of weight from COVID, and now I'm just going back to my old ways. So, please forgive me. And I'd like to apologize to Adele, too."

Now it was Caroline's turn to be still for a moment. "Gee, Reggie, I don't know what to say, other than, you're amazing. Of course, you can eat anything you want, but being sensitive to my needs is awesome. Thank you."

"Thank you for not being angry," he said. He leaned over and kissed her, followed by several more kisses.

"What about the food funeral?" she asked, breaking the moment.

"Of course, I'll officiate. It's something to add to my resume," he said, smiling. "Let's set a date, and we'll get it done." They left the park, hand in hand.

The funeral was planned for two days later. On the day of the event, Caroline rummaged through her cupboards, and hiding places, and came up with a large bag of forbidden treats. They drove to her favorite fast-food spots, and placed her orders. The aromas in the car were sinful and excruciatingly painful. It took tremendous willpower not to reach into one of the bags and grab a handful of hot, salty fries. Before placing the bags of food in the trunk, she liberally sprinkled them with Ajax Cleanser. Reggie's admiration and respect for Caroline grew as she drove from restaurant to restaurant, and placed the bags of detergent-covered food in the trunk. "If they're in the backseat, I'll just reach over and grab food," she admitted.

"You're wonderful, Caroline. You're such a strong, independent woman. And, what a novel idea."

"Thank you," she said smiling back at him.

They drove to Adele's home with their contaminated stash. Adele was waiting for them in the backyard, shovel in hand, standing over a deep hole. Adele greeted Reggie warmly. Obviously, the tension had dissipated. Adele realized she was taking out her fears and pain on him – her silly and outlandish fear that he knew Marcelo, and that he might have sex with Caroline, and repeat the history she had experienced: leaving her pregnant and abandoned. She knew she had no right to impose her personal plights onto an innocent man, who obviously cared about Caroline.

Adele placed a bag of food into the hole. Caroline followed with her bags of food. The two women took turns covering the hole with dirt.

Reggie stood near the plot and paused. Then he gently segued into his eulogy. "During our lives, the most motivating factor is love, which encompasses many things. We love our family, friends, pets and sometimes even inanimate objects, such as a favorite dress, a trinket, or a piece of jewelry. But as we know, people and pets eventually die, leaving us with only our memories, most of them positive reminders, others palpably painful.

"When the love of certain foods become our constant companion, and a destructive force, we must say goodbye to that which was once our greatest obsession. Such an addiction, which for you is junk food, has derailed you in many ways. Because it has, it is time to abandon it, and to never allow such damaging demons into your life again. Caroline and Adele, today is a time of letting go. It is a time to find relief and renewal in knowing that these foods will no longer bring temptation, suffering and unhealthy habits into your lives. Look at them as foods you are severely allergic to, that will bring you great physical harm if ingested.

"And so, while we now release you from the control that certain foods had over you, now, and forever more, we relegate your unhealthy edibles, and their associated cravings, to their final resting place. Amen."

Together, Caroline and Adele echoed, "Amen."

Afterwards, the three walked back into Adele's house and replaced their face masks. Their conversation was relaxed, and more open than the first time they met. Reggie spoke about his numerous Internet certifications, which Adele found very amusing. He told her about his parents, both in their early sixties, and how they were working from home. They had lost several friends in their fifty-five and older community. "It's shocking," he said, "how many people believe this virus is a hoax. I spent a week in the hospital. This is a devastating and dangerous disease, not just a seasonal flu."

When Caroline excused herself to accept a phone call from work, Reggie used the opportunity to ask, "Adele, I can see how close you two are, so I hope you won't mind if I ask you a personal question."

Adele's heart began pounding. *Did he notice the resemblance? Was he going to ask if she was Caroline's mother?*

"Sure," she murmured.

"I'd like to ask your permission for Caroline's hand in marriage."

Adele was stunned. "I don't know what to say, other than, don't you think you should be asking her father? I mean . . . I'm flattered, but I don't know if it's my place to grant you permission."

"Caroline told me about the difficulties with her parents, and I saw firsthand how nasty her sister was to her. I'd like to discuss this further with you, Adele. Before Caroline returns, can you AirDrop your number to my cell?" He promised to text her when Caroline was working.

Adele was touched. She realized what a special guy he was, after all. Her apprehensions quickly dissolved. "Reggie, I really don't know you, but from what I've seen, Caroline cares a lot about you. And you seem enamored with her. I'd say that the two of you need to get to know each other better. I don't want either of you getting hurt."

"Of course, Adele. I would never do anything to hurt Caroline. She's an amazing woman."

Their conversation was cut short when Caroline returned to the room. They left after sharing cups of coffee, sans dessert, and feeling lighter of heart.

Reggie didn't sleep on the air mattress that evening.

Thirty Three

"Hi Marc. It's Simone."

"Sim-Sim," Marc Rosenzweig chirped into the phone. "How are you? Are you and Charlie doing okay during this crazy pandemic?"

"We're doing very well, thank you. Charlie and I became parents of twins in August, a boy and a girl. Mrs. Smith and Irene moved in next door, and they take care of the babies while Charlie and I try to keep our businesses afloat. How are you and the family?"

"Congratulations. I'm sure buttons are popping off Charlie's vest," he said jokingly. "The family is well," he continued. "But we had a scare back in November. My mother contracted COVID and she was in the hospital for a month. She's home now. This virus is awful, Simone. We've lost several friends."

"Us, too," Simone said. But quickly segueing into the purpose of her call, she said, "Marc, I'm wondering if you can look into something for me. I have a client who is intent on marrying herself."

"Are you joking, Simone?" he asked. "I've never heard of such a thing."

"It's a long story. Her name is Caroline Olivia Wight. Her sister despises her, and even went so far as to push her into a body of water when they were in Florida . . . and within range of a crocodile. I'd like to investigate Caroline's background. There's something fishy about this family. Maybe it's none of my business, but curiosity has gotten the better of me."

Simone continued filling Marc in on Caroline with as much information as she had. Marc Rosenzweig, a private investigator from New Jersey, had done extensive work for Simone. She and Jennifer were the event planners for his son's and daughter's respective Bar and Bat Mitzvahs. Several years later, when his daughter got engaged, Simone and Jennifer organized her engagement party. Then, her bridal shower and ultimate wedding. That was followed a few years later with his son's wedding. Subsequently, they also planned Marc and his wife's twenty-fifth wedding anniversary, and multiple birthday parties for their kids and grandkids. Their relationship spanned years.

"I'll get back to you as soon as I can," Marc said. "Believe it or not, during the pandemic when couples are stuck at home with each other, suspicions become elevated. It seems one can't even go into another room to call a lover, without their spouse finding out," he joked. "It's an interesting time, Simone. I'm not complaining, it's just strange."

"And asking you to investigate a woman who wants to marry herself just goes along with the rest it," Simone said, humorously.

"It certainly does. Give my best to Charlie. And congratulations again on the birth of your twins. I wish I could have been at the bris," he chuckled.

"It's too late, Marc. The drastic deed was performed in the hospital. Be well. Stay masked."

Three days later, Marc called Simone back with an update.

"I found Caroline's birth certificate. Evelyn Taormina Wight is listed as her mother, and Sean Franklin Wight as the father. I also found adoption papers."

"Adoption papers?" Simone asked, her curiosity piqued.

"Yes. It seems Caroline was born out of wedlock. The original birth certificate, which was amended to list Evelyn and Sean as her parents, is held by the state registrar of vital records. It's supposed to be kept confidential, but these days with so many people searching for their birth parents, it's easy to obtain confidential information. Her adoption was not a 'closed adoption' meaning Caroline could have researched this information when she turned eighteen."

"Adopted," Simone muttered.

"Her birth mother was listed as Adele Taormina, and the father as Marcelo Pérez." She was born in a now defunct maternity home in Rochester, NY, run by the Sisters of Perpetual Help."

"Wow. I suspected Caroline was adopted, but never put the pieces of the puzzle together. Adele is Caroline's mother's sister."

"It's not the first time I've come across this, Simone. Many times, to save embarrassment, an older sister will take in the child and raise him or her as their own. It appears this is what's happened here. I hope this helps."

"Yes . . . yes, of course. It helps tremendously." Pondering another thought, she asked, "Marc, are you able to research someone's will? Would Adele's will be public knowledge? I'm curious as to whom would be the beneficiary of her estate."

"Unfortunately, unless Adele passes away, and her will goes through probate, that's not public information."

They ended their conversation with the usual pleasantries.

Back at Simone's house, all was quiet. The babies were napping, and Mrs. Smith and Irene were doing laundry. Simone sat on the sofa, a glass of pinot grigio nearby, as she looked out on Long Island Sound just a stone's throw from the house. The sun was setting, the sky was filled with streaks of vibrant yellow, orange and red. The water was calm, unlike the lives around her. She thought about what she should do with this information. *Interesting,* she thought. *This answers a lot of questions . . . why Wanda dislikes her sister, why Caroline went back to the wedding site to collect a cigarette butt . . .* But Simone decided this wasn't her secret to tell. She wondered if Caroline suspected she was adopted, or knew that Adele was really her biological mother.

Simone suddenly felt tired. She flipped on the gas fireplace, grabbed the throw blanket nearby, and within minutes she drifted off to sleep.

Thirty Four

After the night of Caroline's first sexual experience, she stumbled to the kitchen to brew a pot of coffee, and make toast. She was starving, and very thirsty. She put food down for her dog, opened the refrigerator and poured a large glass of orange juice. She had no regrets for the decision she had made inviting Reggie into her bed. She suddenly felt like a fully blossomed woman. She was lost in thought when Reggie came up behind her and began kissing her neck. She closed her eyes and took in the wave of new sexual desires that washed over her. She turned to face him, and they offered each other mutually passionate kisses.

"Come back to bed," he whispered.

She eagerly accepted his request.

It was eleven o'clock when Caroline turned on her computer. She had hours of work to catch up on, but her time with Reggie quickly erased any guilty feelings. Her email in-box had the two communications she had been anxiously awaiting: the results of her DNA, and news of her ancestry. The words jumped out at her, muddled her thinking, and shook the very core of her being. "Lies . . . all fabricated lies," she said out loud. Certainly, there had to be a mistake.

The lipstick stain on the cigarette butt showed a familiar connection, but not a foolproof one. She and her sister were related, but they did not have the same parents. Her DNA results were also filled with falsehoods. She was part Italian, and part Cuban. *How could this be?* she thought.

"Reggie, can you come in here, please," she shouted from her office. "Look at these emails. If you remember, on the day of the ceremony, Wanda was smoking a cigarette. When you took us back to the venue to retrieve Jennifer's handbag, I picked up my sister's used cigarette butt. I sent it in for DNA testing." She pointed to the computer screen. "She and I are not officially related."

Then, opening the ancestry email, Reggie said, "Cuban? Who in your family is Cuban?"

"No one that I know of," she said. "Do you understand what this means, Reggie?" Caroline turned to face him. "It means that my mother, who is from Italy, had an affair with a Cuban man."

She turned back to the email, and read it again, looking for an incorrect name, or another notation that proved the results were erroneous. "I wonder if my father knows," she said shocked by the fact that all this time, the man she believed to be her father, actually was another man.

"What are you going to do with this information?" Reggie asked.

"I don't know. I feel sick," Caroline said, and walked away from the horrors emanating from the computer screen.

"Maybe Adele knows," Reggie suggested.

"She might, but I can't ask her, especially if she had promised my mother to keep it a secret. Then again, maybe my mother never told her sister that she had had an affair."

"Caroline, is it possible that your mother was raped?"

"I never thought of that," she said, horrified, his words upending her thinking process. "I have to compile more information, but I don't know whom to ask."

"Do you have a copy of your birth certificate?"

Caroline rummaged through her closet until she found a small metal box with her important papers: cash, the title to her car, her passport and birth certificate. She read out loud: "Mother: Evelyn Taormina Wight. Father: Sean Franklin Wight."

She began sobbing. "I don't know who I am anymore. This birth certificate is obviously a fake."

Reggie put his arms around her, holding her tightly. He had no words of comfort or suggestions. He felt as equally lost as she did.

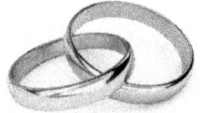

Thirty Five

Caroline couldn't focus on work. She sent her boss an email saying she needed to take a personal day. She promised to make it up over the next week. Production on an audio book was ahead of schedule, so her boss didn't give her a hard time. Caroline realized she had no friends in whom to confide. The only available person was her aunt, but she wasn't about to discuss her mother's infidelity with her. She needed to clear her mind. She and Reggie took Pyewacket for a long walk in the park. She discussed her options, which finally came down to confronting her mother, or asking her aunt.

She stopped abruptly, faced Reggie, and said, "Do you remember Wanda screaming and telling me that she convinced them to take me in? I bet she knows something. But she's such a bitch, I wouldn't give her the satisfaction of thinking she had something on me. I'm completely out of ideas."

They sat down on a bench. Pye jumped up onto Caroline's lap, and immediately fell asleep.

"I guess we kept him up all night," Reggie said, trying to lighten the mood.

Caroline looked adoringly at Reggie, her eyes sparkling with affection towards this incredible man. *To think,* she mused, *last year I was convinced I'd never find someone to love . . . or someone to love me back . . . was it even possible,* she wondered.

"Caroline, I remember seeing you and Jennifer acting like pretty good friends, especially when you were in the hospital. The two of you hung out a lot. Maybe she can offer you some guidance."

"That's a fantastic idea, Reggie," Caroline agreed.

She dug into her purse, pulled out her cell phone, and called Jennifer. She explained the discovery of her ancestry, and asked if she, or Simone, had any suggestions.

"I know Simone has worked with a private investigator in New Jersey," Jennifer said. "Maybe he can help you. I'll ask Simone to text you his contact info."

Within the hour, Caroline was on the phone with Marc Rosenzweig, enlightening him with all the details. "Simone and Jennifer highly recommended you," she said. "Can you do any further in-depth research on the subject?"

Marc promised to get back to her when he procured more information. "But I need to know, Ms. Wight, are you sure you are willing to hear about everything I find? The truth can be very difficult to assimilate."

"I think so," Caroline said, hesitating slightly. "Like what kind of information?"

"In my line of business, I find all sorts of things . . . police records, infidelities, sexual assaults. But let me be clear, Ms. Wight, I might not find out anything. I just need to know the boundaries, and what you're prepared to hear."

"I want to know everything, Mr. Rosenzweig," Caroline assured him. "Everything."

They hung up, and Marc immediately called Simone. "We have a situation," he said dropping their usual banter, and staying focused on the task at hand.

"What's up, Marc" Simone said, equally concerned.

"I just got off the phone with Caroline Olivia Wight. The same woman you asked me to investigate. She wants me to look into her background. I did more digging on Marcelo Pérez. He's a rapist, and a murderer. He's been in jail for the past ten years, doing a life sentence. Apparently, someone's husband came home early, caught his wife in bed with Pérez, and the two men fought. Pérez killed the husband, then violently raped the woman, although they had been having an affair. He told her he'd kill her, too, if she identified him. The police found Pérez's DNA in the bedroom, and the woman broke down and told the police the whole story."

"Why is this a situation, Marc?" Simone asked.

"I asked her if she wants me to report everything I find. I think it's going to be enough of a shock to learn Pérez is her biological father, but do I tell her about his history of brutality? I know studies can vary, but when someone in the family has violent tendencies, these genes could be hereditary. Some say it's nature vs. nurture. But if Caroline were to have children, these biological traits and propensities might be passed down."

"If Caroline said she wants to know everything, then tell her," Simone said. "But please do not reveal that I asked you to do a background check on her."

"You have my word, Simone. Since I already have a lot of the information, it will be easy for me to give her a full report."

"And, you know, Marc, if you don't tell her about her father's violence, she might go looking for him, and discover it herself. That could open up a real can of worms."

"This is the part of my job I don't like," Marc said. "Thanks for trusting me, Simone. I'll try to present my findings to Ms. Wight as gently as possible."

Three days later, and due to the pandemic, Marc invited Caroline to a Zoom meeting. Introductions were made virtually. Reggie, who sat by her side, held her hand during the entire meeting.

His research yielded photographs of Adele, Marcelo Pérez, Caroline's birth certificate and adoption papers. Adele's information was easy to find as she was a Superintendent of Schools. He got Marcelo's prison photo, and found on social media, several photos of Marcelo with his wife and children. He scanned all of it, and sent it on to Caroline.

"So, you see, Ms. Wight," Marc concluded, "your aunt is your biological mother. You were born in upstate New York at a maternity home, and your biological father is Marcelo Pérez. When you were born," he continued, "abortions were still taboo, and I assume your family is Catholic, making it a mortal sin. Has your aunt ever spoken of this man?"

"No," Caroline said, "but once I overheard a whispered conversation about a man who broke my aunt's heart. Maybe it was this Marcelo guy. I should say, my father."

"Ms. Wight," Marc said in an even tone, "you're not the first person to be adopted. Your true parents are the ones who raised you . . . changed your diapers, sat up with you when you were sick, fed and clothed you. Ms. Wight, you're fortunate that your aunt is in your life, and that your biological mother is not a complete mystery. That must provide some solace for you."

"I suppose," she said solemnly. "Now I know why I don't look anything like my sister. I was always told I take after my grandfather, who was short and stocky. But when I view Aunt Adele's professional photo, I can see a striking resemblance. I never realized it before. I wonder if others saw that, too."

"I did," Reggie said. "I mentioned it the first time I met your aunt."

"Yes, you did. I didn't think anything of it at the time."

"I want you to think about this, Ms. Wight. Consider your aunt's situation, and the turmoil she went through. Her heart must break every time she sees you. It couldn't have been easy to watch her sister raise you as her own. I'm sure there were many times she wanted to hold you, and call you her daughter. I hope in time you can be empathetic. Try to understand her plight."

"I will try," Caroline said.

She turned to Reggie, "Now I understand why she was upset about you staying in my apartment. She probably feared you'd get me pregnant and then abandon me. She thought I might repeat history."

Looking back at the investigator she asked, "What about my father? What's his story?"

"According to my investigation, he was almost twice Adele's age at the time you were conceived. His rap sheet shows several alleged rapes, but when the women were to testify, they changed their story, and said the sex was consensual. This might have happened to your aunt, who was only sixteen at the time. He is in jail now, and probably will never see the light of day again."

"Which jail is he in?"

"A state prison in Miami."

"Miami!" Caroline shouted.

"Is something wrong?" he asked, knowing full well the story of Caroline's sister pushing her into the water in Key Biscayne.

"No . . . no . . . I'm sorry. It's just that Reggie is from the Miami area. I think I'm just overwhelmed with all this information."

They ended their conversation, leaving Caroline confused, and angry. Although she knew it wasn't a fair emotion, she felt suddenly abandoned.

She turned to Reggie, and asked, "Would you mind if I go off by myself for a little while? I need some time alone."

"Sure, I understand. But promise me, Caroline, you're

not going to hit a fast-food drive through, and give up on your diet."

"I won't. I promise."

Caroline left Reggie in the apartment, and drove the six miles to her destination. She sat in her car for five minutes, still unsure of her mission. Finally, she got out and walked to the door of the house.

A woman opened her front door to find Caroline standing there.

"Hello, Mother."

Thirty Six

August 2020

The virus raged on. Deaths in the United States continued to skyrocket with no end in sight. Simone's office, as well as numerous other companies, restaurants and bars were closed to the public. She and Jennifer coordinated collecting mail at the office. As the months went on, trips to the office dwindled down to once every three weeks.

Simone paid her employees one-hundred percent of their salary, until they were able to collect unemployment. Then, she supported them by matching the difference. Although this was a financial burden, she knew that once the pandemic ended, her business would be up and running at full capacity, replenishing her emergency fund. The silver lining, if one existed, was that she and Charlie both worked primarily from home, allowing them to spend quality time with their now one-year-old children.

It was a warm Monday evening in early August. Charlie had endured another difficult day at work. He arrived that morning for a family meeting to discuss the direction, and future of the hotel. The Grand Hamilton Hotel had been in the family for three generations, and without warning or foresight, it now looked as if it would have to shut its doors forever.

Fifteen family members, and senior staff sat in the grand ballroom, six feet apart from each other. No welcoming hugs, kisses or handshakes were exchanged. The family had not been together since mid-February. Their spouses and children were sheltered inside their homes, just like most of America, which was on lockdown.

"We have enough capital to keep the old place running for another two months," Charles, Senior announced as he brought the meeting to order. "The small outside gatherings we are allowed to have is what's saving us. But we're not up to the usual *Hamilton* standards," he said with a commanding voice that echoed throughout the room.

"No one is up to their standards, dad," Charlie's sister, Harriet said. "Imagine places like Tiffany's and Cartier are suffering too, including all the restaurants that have shut their doors for good. Family businesses that have been around for generations are gone. They've lost everything."

"We're not *Tiffany's*," her father said sternly. "We're the *Grand Hamilton*, one of the most prestigious hotels on Connecticut's Gold Coast. We've made it through worse times." He continued pontificating, as if completely oblivious to what was happening to other establishments. Charlie began doodling on his notepad while his father, a windbag and boaster, went on about how successful the family business was in its day. His ramblings drifted on until the others began yawning.

Charlie reintroduced the idea of building a covered portico on the side of the hotel. Since gatherings of twenty or fewer were allowed, especially outdoors, they could now create smaller, and more intimate events, with little concern or exposure to weather. At the first suggestion, his father dismissed the idea. "We're trying to save money, Charlie, not spend it." But this time, the others applauded the proposal, and were willing to give up some of the hotel's capital to have a portico built.

The meeting lasted for two hours. By its end, Charlie's head was pounding. He went to his office, closed the door, and took a much-needed twenty-minute nap. He popped a couple of Advil with his coffee - his fifth cup that day - and got to work. He kept in touch with clients whose events or business conferences had been canceled. He wanted them to know the hotel was still in business. They brainstormed various options on newly-designed conferences using Zoom, or other social media outlets. He encouraged couples, contracted to have their wedding at the hotel, to create intimate weddings, instead of their original guest list of two or three hundred guests. He never referred them to Simone, as they both felt that would be a conflict of interest. If an engaged couple asked for the name of a wedding planner, Charlie provided three names of professional planners, allowing the couple to choose their own planner to help with their wedding.

At the end of the day, while Charlie drove home, he thought about how much his life had changed over the past year. He was now a father of twins, who brought him tremendous joy. He was also surrounded by women, now that Mrs. Smith and Irene lived next door. He craved the times he and few of his buddies went to a Yankees game, or watched football at one of their homes. He wondered how much longer the social distancing was going to last. It had become torturous for everyone.

He stopped to pick up dinner. He and Simone were planning to celebrate the twins' one-year birthday with a special meal for the family. When he read the sign on the restaurant door, he wept openly and unabashedly. This news came at the end of a stressful day, a nerve wracking time, not only in his life, but for those around him. Everyone he knew was dealing with the same gnawing anxiety and uncertainty as he was. It was apoplectic in scope, and no one knew when a vaccine would become available. The unknown loomed ahead like a dark cloud under which people moved about in states of abysmal uncertainty.

When Simone saw her husband's face, she knew something was terribly wrong. "What is it, Charlie? You look awful."

"I have some terrible news," he started. "I think you should sit down."

Charlie walked over to the bar and poured himself a scotch, which he drank down in one quick slug. He poured another, walked back to the sofa and sat down next to Simone.

"DaPietro's closed because of COVID-19," he suddenly blurted out.

Simone was stunned and silent. No words, no feelings, no reaction. She just stared at Charlie. Finally, she whispered, "But that can't be. Maybe they're closed for vacation."

"No," Charlie sadly assured her. "The sign said that after thirty years, Pietro was forced to close because of the pandemic. The building is also up for sale."

At that moment, it occurred to Simone the severity of what was happening right outside her own front door. She was busy every day with the babies, and her "social life" consisted of her husband, the twins, and their caretakers. She had enough people around her to satisfy her needs. She did video conference calls with Jennifer every day, so she "saw" her, and talked to clients on a regular basis. Her life kept going, without a hiccup. But the others – how could she have been so blind?

"Charlie, I feel as if a family member just died. I must call Pietro's wife, Janine, to express our condolences and support. I can't imagine what they must be going through. It's so sad, so disheartening."

DaPietro's was just another example of what the pandemic was doing to America, and other countries around the world.

Simone put her head on her husband's shoulder and together they wept.

Thirty Seven

"Simone, Simone," Jennifer shouted into the phone. "You're not going to believe what just happened."

"Calm down," Simone said to her friend and partner. "Catch your breath, and tell me what's going on."

"Remember Dr. Brady . . . Mike Brady?"

"Dreamy eyes? Yeah, I remember him," Simone said, teasing.

"He's moving to Boston, and he wants me to join him. He asked me to move in with him."

Simone was shocked, and she feared Jennifer was once again acting impulsively, a trait that had gotten her into trouble in the past. She couldn't find the appropriate words to express her feelings.

"Are you still there?" Jennifer asked.

"I'm here," Simone said. "I'm just a bit stunned by the news. When is this going to happen?" Simone held her breath hoping Jennifer wasn't going to abandon her position at the company, and leave next week.

"Well, I told him I had to talk to you. After all, my first commitment is to you, Simone."

"Thank you. How did all this come about?"

"Mike was offered a teaching position at Harvard, his alma mater. He plans to move after Christmas."

Simone chose her words carefully. She and Jennifer had had their disagreements in the past, one that had forced Jennifer to leave the company for over a year. If she were to leave, it could sever their friendship, again. Jennifer was a major asset to "I Do" and to Simone. But she was also entitled to live her own life, and Simone shouldn't be the one to stop her.

"I didn't know you and Mike were dating."

"We've been dating virtually. Because of COVID, and Mike being exposed on a daily basis, we only see each other online. We talk every evening on Skype."

"I had no idea. I've been so busy with the twins, being a new mom, trying to keep the business afloat . . . all excuses, Jennifer. I'm sorry I haven't asked you about Mike since the last time we saw him."

"I'm sorry, too, that I haven't said anything to you. I had to be sure I wanted to get into another relationship. After my failed marriages, and Anthony leaving me at Charles Island . . . well, Mike isn't like any of them. He's a gentleman, a successful doctor, and Simone, he loves me. He truly loves me," Jennifer gushed. "He loves me more than any other man has ever loved me."

Again, being careful with her sentiments, Simone simply said, "I'm very happy for you, Jennifer. After all you've been through these past years, and having your mom and brother dying recently. Well, you deserve some happiness."

"Do you really mean that, Simone?"

"I do."

The two women laughed at those words. How often they've said them when announcing the name of the company, or hearing couples promising themselves to each other.

"Will you be moving in with him soon?"

"I don't know. Like I said, I wanted to discuss this with you first, before giving him my final answer."

"Jennifer, it's your life. You have to decide – not me. I will miss you terribly. You've been a close friend, business partner, and aunt to my babies. But I cannot make up your mind for you. It's obvious Mike cares about you, and wants you in his life.

"Simone," Jennifer said, "I haven't any family. Sure, I consider you, Charlie and the twins my family, but I want one of my own someday. I'm not getting any younger, and I see a bright future with Mike. But I feel guilty leaving the company again," she said sincerely.

"I understand, Jennifer. You need to plan your future. Most importantly, go with your heart. I don't know how to say this, but has Mike made a promise to you? You know, a future, a marriage proposal?" Simone began to stammer, and searched for the right words.

"Simone," Jennifer said, "please, don't fret. I know you're worried I'll make another mistake, like I did with Anthony, always saying we'd get married, but never actually setting a date. Mike and I have discussed our future together. He needs to get settled in Boston. After a year, we'll buy a house, and get married."

"Jennifer, you two will figure out your life together. You don't need my approval."

"I know that," Jennifer said.

"You and I have seen what happens to couples who 'play house' only to discover it's not all that wonderful."

"Yes, I know, Simone. I was thinking the same thing. I thought about the couple from New Rochelle who bought a house together, and never created any legal documents to protect themselves before the marriage. They went through all the wedding plans, but when they sat down and discussed what they wanted for their future, they realized they were on two separate paths. She lost her investment in the house, and they ended up in a nasty court battle."

"Yes, I remember Andy and Andi. I think they were more in love with their matching names than with each other. Do you remember his reaction when, during our consultation, I suggested they discuss having children? And what would happen if they weren't able to conceive? Would they consider adopting?"

"Yes, he went nuts when you said that," Jennifer recalled.

"All I wanted for them was to discuss how they felt about having children. I never suggested they discuss the subject with us. But he got so defensive. I felt bad for Andi. I thought she was a sweet young woman, but very naïve and immature. It's too bad they couldn't make a go of it."

"Simone," Jennifer said, becoming serious, and trying to move the conversation back to her and Mike, "will you be very upset if I leave "I Do" and go to Boston to live with Mike?"

"Naturally, I will miss you, but no, of course not," Simone said. "Just use good judgment before making a commitment to move from Connecticut. And, please think about what you'll do for work once you get settled."

The two continued their conversation about the company, the twins, and the latest news on the virus. They decided to do a Zoom call to discuss in detail Jennifer's move to Boston, and whom Simone could hire to replace her.

Meanwhile, Simone considered her options. She had several professional planners in her office, but would any of them be a good replacement for Jennifer? First, she considered Cindy, an Asian-American millennial who increased Simone's business by twenty percent. Cindy had numerous connections in Chinatown and Queens, New York. But her professionalism left a lot to be desired. For the first several months while working at "I Do," Cindy came to work in tank tops, cut offs and revealing yoga pants. Simone dropped hints about her appearance, but Cindy never got the message. It wasn't until Simone had a meeting with Cindy, and told her that her attire was far from appropriate, that the young woman changed her appearance to a more professional image.

Since COVID-19, which originated in China, Cindy's business had dried up. Fear of retaliation by anti-Asians forced many Asians to keep a very low profile. Simone had difficulty reaching Cindy, calling or texting several times before she would respond to Simone. The concluding decision was that Cindy would not be a good fit for moving up in the company.

Another planner, Gary ("GG") was quick to argue. He defended every design idea he presented. He and Cindy were like oil and water, and Simone could not have them working together unless Jennifer was referee. Gary was in charge of designing extravagant venues, with the latest floral and theme designs. He was creative, ambitious and a hard worker. Simone worked well with him, but many others, both in her office and in the industry, found his attitude off-putting. Simone felt that he, too, wasn't a good fit for an administrative position.

There were others in the office, but none seemed to be what Simone needed to grow her company once the pandemic ended. She finally called Leslie, her former intern.

"How did the wedding go in Monte Carlo?" Simone asked her.

"I was jet lagged for a week, Simone," Leslie said. "The wedding was beautiful and extravagant. I was lucky to be part of the team of ten planners."

"Ten!" Simone exclaimed.

"There were over one thousand people in attendance. It was truly a once-in-a-lifetime experience. I'm glad it's over. Now, back to the ho-hum three-hundred-person weddings," Leslie chuckled.

"I agree," Simone said. Focusing on the reason for her call, she added, "Leslie, I'd like to talk to you about coming back to "I Do." It appears that Jennifer is leaving, and I think the timing for you is good. I could use someone with your experience and energy."

"I'm surprised Jennifer is jumping ship again," Leslie said.

"It's for a good reason this time," Simone quickly interjected. It wasn't Simone's place to give Leslie a full explanation of Jennifer's decision. If Jennifer wanted others to know why she was leaving the company, she could tell them. Until then, she wasn't going to indulge in gossip. "I don't think she's going to be leaving until the end of this year. Since COVID shut down my business, it will be at least six to nine months before I'll be up and running again, possibly late 2021, or 2022."

Leslie was silent while Simone went on about how she feared one or two of her planners would not return after she reopened. "I think people, who have held off getting married are going to be planning an extra spectacular wedding, especially if they've had over a year to save more money. Others, I'm sure, have blown through their wedding money just to survive. Regardless, though, I'm hoping to see business boom in the future," Simone said optimistically. "What do you think, Leslie? Are you interested?"

"I'd have to give this some serious thought, Simone. I'm flattered you'd consider asking me to return. I enjoyed working with you the year I interned at your company." She carefully phrased her next question. "Simone, I know at one time you and Jennifer were financial partners. Would you ever consider that possibility again?"

"I'd be happy to give it some consideration, Leslie. But I have to admit, I've been carrying the company since the shutdown, and I've invested lots of money. I'd have to discuss this idea with my financial advisor."

"Of course," Leslie said. "Hey, you can't be told 'no' unless you ask."

"It seems I taught you well," Simone laughed.

"That you did."

"How about we have a Zoom call in two weeks? Meanwhile, consider what it will take to get you to move back to Connecticut. I'm sure we can come up with a workable compromise."

"Is GG still working for you?" Leslie asked.

"Yes, he is. But he only does design work. Would he influence your decision?" Simone asked.

"No," she answered. Taking some time to respond, she added, "But we'd have to establish boundaries. I've worked with him in the past, and he's quick to argue, and can get nasty if things aren't done his way."

"I know. I've seen him in action. But he's much better now. It's a matter of stroking his ego."

They ended their call, agreeing to a day and time for a virtual meeting. Simone had a lot of thinking to do. She hadn't planned on bringing in another business partner. She faced a large expense when her partnership with Jennifer was severed a few years ago. She should not add to her expenses, considering she was losing money every day her office was shut down. She'd have to talk to her attorney, financial planner, and Charlie for guidance and advice.

Thirty Eight

Charles "Charlie" Hamilton IV, was next in line to inherit the family business and overseeing one of the largest hotels on the Gold Coast of Connecticut. Unfortunately, Charlie's father treated his son like an incompetent, unmotivated child, and had embarrassed him publicly at staff meetings, and in sessions with customers and family members.

Charlie's sister, Harriet, had pushed her son, Frederick Murphy, to work his way from busboy to assistant banquet manager. Frederick's self-importance dominated his critical thinking and decisions. He had made several bad choices, and felt entitled to spy on his Uncle Charlie's work and private life.

During the time Frederick was working his way up the ladder at the hotel, Charlie's marriage to his first wife, Eve, was falling apart. Frederick took it upon himself to gossip to his grandfather and others about Eve's actions. It seemed everyone knew, except for Charlie, that Eve was having an affair with the tennis instructor. When Frederick suspected a relationship was developing between his uncle and one of the wedding planners, Simone Simpson, he planted listening devices in their hotel rooms, and tried using his surveillance against them. But Charlie was one step ahead of his nephew. After proof of Frederick's inappropriate behavior surfaced in front of a client, he fired Frederick. But Charlie's father, who was head of the hotel, gave in to his daughter Harriet's pleas, and rehired him, much to Charlie's chagrin.

These days, Frederick, like the other employees at the hotel, was working from home. He and other senior staff members rotated overseeing the hotel. They were required to sanitize all surfaces before sitting down at a desk, staying a minimum of six-feet apart, and wearing CDC-approved masks.

Charlie was in his home office, brainstorming ideas for when the hotel would be up to running at full capacity. Given that business was off by over 80% during the last year, he didn't know where the money was going to come from to support these creative ideas. But he wanted to get them down on paper before they disappeared from his mind. Suddenly, his cell rang, startling him.

"Charles," his mother said on the phone. Charlie immediately knew by her flat tone that something was wrong.

"Hello, Mother. Is everything okay?"

"Your father is in the hospital . . . he's intubated . . . he's dying, Charles. He's dying." His mother began sobbing on the phone. She was a stoic woman, who had lived through many challenges over their fifty years of marriage. Charlie knew about his father's extramarital affairs; and each time his mother had turned a blind eye. His father was an arrogant bore who loved hearing the sound of his own voice. Ironically now, that voice was silenced by a tube.

"When did this happen, Mother?"

"Your father hadn't been feeling well for the past week. He refused to go to the doctor. Last night he collapsed while walking into the kitchen, and was rushed to Greenwich Hospital. He has COVID, and according to the doctor, his chance of survival is very low."

"I'm sorry to hear this, Mother. Is there anything I can do?" Charlie asked. He realized his heart was devoid of empathy for his father's condition.

"There's nothing any of us can do. They won't let me see him. If he dies, he'll be alone."

"Mother, I wish I could come over to be with you, but as you know, you might be infected, too. And with the babies . . ."

"No, you stay home with your family. Harriet said she'll stop by later with food, and she'll take my vitals. It's nice having a nurse in the family. I only wish your father had listened to Harriet last weekend when he first started to feel ill."

"Please call me if you need anything," Charlie said. "Keep us updated. And Mother," he said earnestly, "I love you. Please take care of yourself."

"I love you, too, son." And she hung up.

Over the past two years, Charlie had developed plans to leave the family business. He no longer wanted to work in the hospitality business, especially under his father's jurisdiction. Every idea Charlie presented to him was dismissed as "pie in the sky" thinking. Charlie felt the hotel should be a family-oriented destination, with family activities. Children could be at a kids' cove while their parents attended conferences. But his father felt these ideas would turn the hotel into a low-class hangout for teenagers. No matter how creative or progressive Charlie's ideas were, his father rejected them.

Charlie knew that business travel wasn't the same as it was during his father's generation. Then, business professionals dressed for conferences in suits and ties, attended on-site vendor programs, and were often away from home for days at a time. Now, it was less formal with more online conferencing and networking rather than in person. Charlie didn't see business meetings returning to the archaic ways during his father's reign. He believed 'business casual' was here to stay, and the way of the future.

Charlie's vision was to bring the entire family to the hotel, and bring back the interactions amongst professionals. Businesses no longer were willing to pay an exorbitant amount for an overnight stay for only one person. It was Charlie's desire to keep the hotel prices the same, or slightly higher, but include the whole family, making the business trip cost-effective. His father wouldn't hear of any of it, although some of the hotel Board members supported Charlie's way of thinking. But his father always had the last word. "I don't want to discuss it," was his usual way of dropping the subject.

Charlie attended night school to obtain his Master's Degree in Business. He graduated in May of 2018, and had planned to slowly separate himself from the Grand

Hamilton Hotel. He thought maybe being Mr. Mom for a year or two would be a good break from the corporate world. He could no longer deal with the hotel politics, his father's constant criticism of him, his life and ideas, and how his sister, Harriet, was pushing for her son, Frederick, to take over Charlie's job. He left his home office to find Simone.

"My father is in ICU on a ventilator," he said casually. "The doctors don't think he's going to make it."

"Oh my. I'm sorry. Is there anything we can do?" Simone asked.

"No, there isn't. My mother might be infected, so we have to stay away. The sad thing is that she can't be with him."

Simone sat quietly next to her husband, studying his face. His jaw was set, his eyes dark, making it impossible to know what he was thinking, or feeling. His relationship with his father had been strained since Charlie was a young child. She could only imagine his internal struggle.

Finally, he spoke. "The timing is awful, Simone. I thought I'd be able to get out of the hotel business. First, the pandemic, and now, if my father dies, I'm going to be stuck running it all."

"What about Frederick? I'm sure your sister would see this as an opportunity to get her son moved up in the ranks. If you take over your father's position, Frederick can take over yours. It might be a golden opportunity, Charlie, for you to create some of the plans you've been wanting to implement for years."

"Yes, that's true, Simone. I hadn't thought of that."

"Maybe he'll recover," she said encouragingly.

"Maybe," Charlie said as he stared out at the water across the way. "Or maybe not."

He left Simone and headed to the kitchen to brew some coffee. He stood watching the foamy elixir pour into the cup. His cell rang. It was his sister, Harriet.

"Daddy's dead," she cried into the phone.

Charles Hamilton V died alone, a weak and helpless man. Neither his wife or his children got to say good-bye. He had been a powerful, demanding presence during his life, but now he was unable to even shout orders to the nurses or doctors, or demand to know what decisions were being made on his behalf.

His body was sent to the Medical Examiner in Farmington, Connecticut. An autopsy was performed; results to be sent to the family in several weeks. Mr. Hamilton's body was cremated, and his remains were sent to the local funeral home. The family was not allowed to hold a formal funeral, a memorial, or a graveside ceremony. Not until the pandemic was over.

Mrs. Hamilton walked around her opulent home, void of the commanding voice of her husband. Suddenly, he was gone. No goodbye, no final kiss, or deathbed admissions. She craved to hear, "see you later," his signature words whenever he walked out the door. No chance to hold his hand as he passed from this life. She knew he had feared death because it was something he could not control, couldn't tell to wait until he was ready, or know his final destination. She spent hours sitting in his armchair, looking out the window, hoping it was all a dream and he'd walk up the path to their front door. Her children couldn't comfort her for fear of infecting her, or she infecting them. It wasn't fair. This whole experience – his death, and the death of so many others – was too painful. She knew she wasn't alone, but the emptiness in her heart was palpable, and she imagined no one else could possibly be suffering as she was. She watched the news and read in the newspaper of how thousands were dying each day from this ominous virulent virus. The thought of others feeling her pain was inconceivable. But it was true, and it was her time to realize that the Hamilton Family was not immune to tragedy, pain and suffering.

Three weeks after her father's death, Harriet arrived at her mother's home with a laptop computer. She wrote down instructions how to Zoom with the rest of the family. There were siblings, grandchildren, cousins, friends and the priest she was able to reach out to for comfort. But at the end of the day, when darkness set in, she climbed into an empty bed and cried herself to sleep.

Harriet returned the next day and removed her father's clothes and personal belongings. Charities were not accepting donations, so she stored the items in her basement where she smelled the aroma of her father every time she entered. Although it was jarring, she knew it was more painful for her mother each time she opened her closet and imagined him standing there, his scent surrounding her like a phantom presence no longer within her reach.

Thirty Nine

November 2020

Reggie remained in Caroline's apartment where they fell into a relaxed and natural daily routine, while outside, the virus raged on. Their mutual comfort level surprised them, as well as it did their families. Reggie's parents were immediately put at ease on their Zoom call, though Reggie's father was a bit more reserved and cautious. They couldn't deny or help noting how happy the couple looked together. His mother thanked Caroline for taking such good care of her son while they were apart. Their virtual meetings became a weekly event, and sometimes included sharing a meal during their Internet connections.

"So, Reggie," his father asked, "when are you coming back home to Florida?"

"I don't know, Dad. I guess it all depends on when it's safe to travel again."

"Things are opening up here in Florida, son. We don't have to wear masks, and many of the restaurants and bars are back in business."

"I'm not ready to take any chances. I feel safer up here with Caroline."

His dad added, "Seems to me you could use some sunshine, and some good food. You're looking too thin."

Sitting next to Caroline, Reggie's stature was smaller. Of course, Caroline took his comment as an afront. The unspoken words of, *you have a fat girlfriend*, were implied. Reggie assured Caroline his dad was just concerned that he no longer had a 'Floridian tan.' But she wasn't convinced.

One afternoon, while Caroline was working, Reggie texted Adele, asking if they could talk. He again brought up his wish to marry Caroline, and asked for Adele's approval.

"Don't you think you should be asking her father?"

"I get the sense he's not a fan of my living with Caroline. He's become very quiet during our Zoom lunches on Sundays. He usually keeps his head down, his mouth full of food, and his fork ready for the next bite."

"That's just his way," Adele assured him. "He's a very shy man."

"Given that, I feel it is proper to ask one of the parents for their daughter's hand in marriage, I'm asking you, Adele."

That sentiment resonated loudly, made Adele's heart melt. She began crying. "I'm very touched, Reggie. Of course, I approve of you marrying Caroline . . . my daughter. I couldn't be happier. The two of you are perfect together."

"Thank you, Adele. Or should I say, Aunt Adele?"

"Have you purchased a ring?" she asked.

"No, I haven't. Since I really don't know my way around the area, and most stores are still closed, I was going to wait until the pandemic was over. Do you have any suggestions?"

"My sister, Evelyn, inherited the family home and furnishings," Adele said. "And I was willed everything else, including my grandmother's engagement ring. It's been in the family for several generations. It would please me so much to have Caroline wear it."

"Wow," Reggie said. "That's such a wonderful gesture, Adele. But what about Wanda? Won't she be upset that Caroline gets the ring instead of her?"

"What Wanda doesn't know, won't hurt her," Adele stated. "Besides, Caroline is my daughter, not Wanda. And I know Caroline will keep it in the family."

"Thank you so much. I'm sure she'll be thrilled."

"Let's meet at Starbucks," Adele suggested. "I'll ask Caroline to get the coffees while we hold a table outside, and I'll slip you the ring. I have to admit, Reggie, I feel like a schoolgirl playing hooky. This is all so exciting."

"I have to go," Reggie whispered into the phone. "Caroline just opened her office door." He quickly disconnected the call."

At the next opportunity, Reggie phoned his father in Miami. "Hi, dad. We need to talk."

"It sounds serious, son. Is everything okay? Are you ill? You didn't look well the last time I saw you."

Reggie cut him off abruptly. "I'm fine dad. I'm going to ask Caroline to marry me."

There was a momentary silence on the other end.

"This is quite a shock, Reggie. How well do you know this girl? Don't you think you're rushing into this . . . after all, you've only known her for a few months."

"Dad, I've known Caroline since March. She's good for me, and I'm good for her. I love her. Please, can't you be happy for me?"

"Yes, of course, I'm happy for you. I just want to be sure you're not jumping into this too quickly. Do you have a date in mind?"

"No, I don't. I haven't asked her yet. I wanted to tell you first."

The men ended their conversation on a better note than it had begun. Reggie wasn't asking for permission, or approval. He was simply showing his respect.

Adele, Caroline and Reggie met on an unusually warm November day. Adele asked Caroline to go inside and order the coffees, while she and Reggie secured a table outside. Adele slipped the ring into Reggie's coat pocket. "Good luck," she whispered. "And know that you have my blessings."

Forty

Thanksgiving 2020

During the past few days, Caroline noticed that Reggie seemed distracted and was deeply in thought. Her insecurities began to surface, fearing Reggie had fallen out of love with her, wanting to leave and return to Florida, abandoning her, just like her biological father did. She hesitated asking him, afraid of what the answer might be. But she believed he would have mentioned a change of heart. Early in their relationship, they had promised that they would discuss any issue that arose between them. This was one of those moments, and Caroline feared she'd lose her nerve to ask him what was wrong. But she finally took a deep breath and asked, "Is everything okay, Reggie?"

"Yeah," he said, offering little else as consolation.

"You seem distant. Are you upset with me for any reason?"

Reggie turned and faced Caroline. "Absolutely not. I'm sorry I've been so quiet lately. I'm feeling a bit homesick." In reality, he was anxious about asking Caroline to marry him. Stumbling for a better explanation, he added, "It must be the holiday. Thanksgiving was when my father's family came to my parents' home. We don't see them often, only at weddings, funerals and on Thanksgiving. I guess I'm missing everyone."

"Your family and mine aren't the only ones dealing with this separation, Reggie. Many families are facing this holiday in unconventional ways. This will be the weirdest Thanksgiving I've ever had. Usually, I'm at my parents' house, along with Wanda's family, and several cousins from New Jersey. My mother and aunt cook for days, and we are always eighteen people for dinner. But this year . . . it's entirely different."

"Well, let's make this Thanksgiving a special one, just for us," Reggie suggested.

"That's a great idea. We can figure out a diet-friendly menu," Caroline offered.

"We'll buy a big, fat turkey." Reggie was now enthusiastically caught up in the idea.

Caroline scrunched her nose, telling him her opinion of that idea.

"We'll have leftovers."

Caroline laughed, and agreed. "But I like dark meat, so I have dibs on the legs. For sides, we can make cauliflower mashed potatoes, steamed string beans, and splurge on cornbread stuffing."

"Sounds perfect," Reggie said, giving Caroline a warm hug.

"I'm so happy you're here with me to share the holiday. I hate to think of Aunt Adele alone, unable to be with anyone," she said.

"Let's Zoom with her," Reggie suddenly jumped in. "We can have Thanksgiving with her." He was considering having Adele witness the proposal.

"What about our parents?" Caroline asked. "We can do a large family gathering, without leaving home."

Well, that kills the idea of Adele participating in the proposal, Reggie thought. He'd have to figure out another place and time.

The couple emailed all the family members, and arranged a large Zoom Thanksgiving Dinner for thirty-five guests. Reggie's parents and relatives were included. Everyone thought the idea was perfect.

"Let's also plan a special breakfast, just for the two of us," Reggie continued. "Let's go all out and splurge on pancakes and bacon."

"That sounds very tempting," Caroline said. "I'll approve going off our diets only if you agree not to include syrup on the pancakes, and only two strips of bacon each."

"Agreed!"

Having a partner as a support system emphasized their compatibility, and Caroline didn't minimize how much that contributed to their relationship.

On Thanksgiving morning, Reggie arose before Caroline. He got busy whipping up the pancake batter, cooking the bacon, and putting on a pot of coffee. The smells wafting through the apartment awakened Caroline. She stumbled into the kitchen, looking half asleep. Her hair was a tangled mess, her eyeglasses were slightly askew, and she wore a robe and slippers. "It smells delightfully sinful in here," she mumbled.

Reggie handed her coffee and pulled out a chair. "Please, have a seat."

Caroline, once again, sensed something wasn't right. Reggie sounded strange – almost robot-like. "Is something wrong?"

"No, not really," he stammered. "I'm afraid of what you're going to say."

Caroline placed her mug on the table, girding herself for the onslaught of his words and awaiting the worst. "Reggie, you know you can say anything to me. I promise I won't get upset."

With that, Reggie placed his hand inside his robe pocket, and pulled out a marquise-shaped diamond ring. Then, he got down on one knee and asked, "Caroline Wight, will you marry me?"

Enormous shockwaves washed over her face. Her mouth dropped open and tears began flowing. "Yes! Yes! Yes!" She rushed into Reggie's arms as they cried together from the sheer joy of the moment.

They feasted on their breakfast, including glasses of mimosas. "Reggie, I'm so happy," Caroline said. "The ring is beautiful."

"It belonged to your grandmother. Aunt Adele slipped it to me when we were at Starbucks."

"My, but you're filled with surprises," Caroline said, not able to stop admiring her left-hand finger. "And Aunt Adele, she knew all along?" Suddenly, Caroline looked at

Reggie, alarmed. "What about Wanda? What if she finds out that this is grandma's ring?"

"She doesn't have to know, unless you tell her. Adele told me she inherited all of your grandmother's possessions, except the family home which was left to your mother. Your aunt – I mean, your biological mother - has been holding onto this ring, hoping someday to pass it on to you."

Caroline was again overcome with emotion. "I can't wait to announce our engagement later today. Everyone will be so surprised. And tomorrow, I'm calling Simone Simpson. This time, she'll *really* be planning a wedding."

That afternoon, Reggie and Caroline announced their engagement to fifteen square boxes on their computer screen, to a total of thirty-five people. Glasses clicked, while a litany of congratulatory sentiments streamed through from each Zoom window. Everyone at the gathering seemed happy for the couple, except for one person, who sat quietly at the table, staring at the engaged couple with vitriolic hatred. There were no wishes of happiness for the couple. Instead, there were wishes of heartbreak, physical pain and thoughts of pending death. *Who does Caroline think she is? She's nothing but a big fat cow.*

Forty One

The next morning, Caroline sent a group text to Simone and Jennifer informing them that she and Reggie were engaged. *Please help plan my REAL wedding!* Caroline wrote.

Jennifer immediately responded expressing her happiness for them, and that she would be pleased to discuss their wedding plans. She would coordinate her calendar with Simone, and get back to her.

Simone also texted back, and expressed her congratulatory wishes. They'd get back to her with a mutual time for a meeting. She then called Jennifer. The two brainstormed a few ideas, and decided it would be best, based on past experiences with Caroline and her family, to have one meeting with everyone present. The pandemic was loosening its grip, but still forced social distancing. So, a meeting location would be a challenge.

"The Grand Hamilton Hotel recently installed an outdoor heated tent, Jennifer. Perhaps we can use the space for our meeting," Simone suggested.

"Perfect location," Jennifer agreed. "Maybe Caroline will want to have her reception there, instead of in Florida."

"Caroline also mentioned that because of the pandemic limiting get togethers, only their immediate families would be invited," Simone said. "And Caroline said they'd like to get married soon, and not wait until the pandemic was over or until people were vaccinated."

"I'm available over the next two weeks for a meeting, before going to Boston to look for a house. All of a sudden, the housing market has gone crazy, Simone. Homes are being sold as soon as they come on the market."

"I'm sure you two will find the perfect place. Oh, I hear the babies," Simone said, cutting Jennifer off, not wanting to remember that her friend and business partner would soon be leaving the company.

It was agreed that on Tuesday, December first, all those involved with planning the wedding would meet at the Grand Hamilton Hotel: Caroline, Reggie, Evelyn, Adele and Wanda.

Caroline was glowing. Simone thought it looked as if she had lost lots of weight since they were last together, over a year ago. In fact, Caroline had lost over seventy-five pounds, wanting to lose another twenty-five before reaching her goal. Caroline's family had not been together since the beginning of the pandemic. Their weekly Zoom meetings didn't do Caroline's figure any justice. When her mother, Evelyn, saw her daughter in person, she began crying. "Tears of happiness for you, Caroline," she said. They wanted to hug, but all they could do was bump elbows. Everyone was masked, so the only joy emanated from their eyes.

Simone chatted with Evelyn and Adele, while Caroline and Reggie engaged with Jennifer. The attendees stood feet apart from each other, and talked about wedding ideas, dates, and location.

Caroline then turned to the group and announced, "I don't want to have the wedding in Florida. I'd like to have it close to home."

"I thought you can't have a wedding because of the pandemic. We're not allowed to be together," Adele added.

"Not unless it's in an open area," Jennifer said.

"Well, if it's just us, why not have the wedding at home? If you're willing to wait until the summer, we can have it outside," Evelyn suggested. "We won't be more than a dozen people."

"We don't want to wait," Reggie said, emphatically. "Caroline and I want to marry right away."

Suddenly, Wanda snapped, "Let's get on with this. I don't have all day."

Everyone turned and looked at Wanda sitting in a chair at the head of one of the tables. Her arms were defiantly folded across her chest. Her eyes flashed anger and annoyance.

"Let's take our places," Simone suggested.

"It's about time," Wanda mumbled.

"Wanda," her mother whispered, "control yourself."

Simone quickly brought the meeting to order, before Wanda had another opportunity to destroy this special moment. "Welcome, everyone," Simone said. "Reggie and Caroline, have you decided on a date for the wedding?"

"Don't make it on Christmas or New Year's . . . I'm busy then," Wanda blurted out before the couple could even answer.

"Wanda, what is wrong with you?" Evelyn scolded her daughter. "You're acting like a child. Be quiet, and let Caroline and Reggie plan their wedding as they wish."

"Does he know who he's marrying? Does he know about the big secret?" Wanda said, interrupting Simone again.

All eyes locked on Wanda. Simone was sure that if masks were removed, everyone's jaw would be shockingly agape.

"What does that mean?" Caroline asked. "What secret?"

"It's not for me to tell," Wanda snorted.

"What secret is that?" Evelyn asked. "If you have something to say, Wanda, then say it," her mother demanded.

"You of all people, Mother, ignoring the fact that Caroline is a bastard child," Wanda said, her eyes flashing.

"Enough," Adele said, trying to curtail Wanda's rant. "Enough of this talk. Wanda, you're out of line."

"*I'm* out of line, Aunt Adele? How about *you*? What did you do when you were sixteen that was out of line? Don't act so self-righteous when you've been pretending all along to be the maiden aunt."

"Oh, no," Evelyn suddenly broke into uncontrollable sobs, covering her face with her hands. "No . . . no . . . no."

"Why are you doing this, Wanda?" Caroline asked, walking closer to her. "You've upset Mom and Aunt Adele."

Wanda had assumed that because Caroline and Adele were close, her aunt had probably told her the family secret years ago. "Yeah, but do you know that when Aunt Adele dies, you'll inherit her estate? And you wonder why I'm furious?"

"How do you know that?" her aunt asked, suddenly realizing Wanda must have gone through her personal papers when she was staying in the house last summer. "So, you snooped."

"Yes, I did," Wanda admitted. "And boy, did I find out a lot about you, Aunt Adele. Like, Caroline's not my real sister."

"Don't say that, Wanda," her mother commanded. "She's your sister as much as Caroline is my daughter, too."

Looking directly at Caroline she announced, "Did you know that Adele is really your mother?"

"Yes, I do know," Caroline answered, flatly.

"Wanda, stop," Evelyn demanded.

"You're as much a fool as Caroline," Wanda said to her mother.

"Wanda, what do you mean about Aunt Adele's estate?" Caroline asked, her eyes darting back and forth between her aunt and her sister.

"Don't tell me you don't know, Caroline. If your *real*

mother dies, you get everything," Wanda shouted. "And when you die, he gets everything," she said pointing a finger at Reggie. "A computer geek gets all of her money."

"Please stop this," Evelyn begged again. "I can't stand seeing you two fighting. You're both my daughters."

"Except for Caroline," Wanda said vindictively.

Caroline put a hand on Evelyn's shoulder and said, "I'm lucky, Wanda. I have two mothers who love me very much."

As if watching a movie unfold in slow motion, Wanda walked up to Caroline, pulled her own arm back as if she was about to throw a fast ball to home plate, and with all her might, flung her first in the direction of Caroline's face. But, as she stepped into the punch, Wanda tripped on a chair leg, lost her balance, and fell forward, hitting her head on the conference table. She landed on the floor with a thud, blood pouring from the deep gash on her forehead. She lay there, unconscious.

Jennifer retrieved her phone from her purse and dialed 911, requesting an ambulance to please hurry.

Social distancing became non-existent. The women rushed over to Wanda. Adele checked for a pulse, while Evelyn picked up her daughter's head and cradled her in her lap. Blood continued to pour, soaking her mother's dress. Caroline stood by stoically, unmoving, as if in a trance.

After Wanda was taken away in an ambulance, Caroline and Reggie left the hotel without saying a word to anyone. Her emotions were tinged with fear – or was it guilt - for what to do next.

When the conference room was cleared of the Wight family members, Simone and Jennifer sat there quietly. There were no words, no explanation of what went on. Finally, Simone spoke. "This could have been a lot worse."

"How?" Jennifer asked.

"What if Wanda landed her punch on the intended target?" Simone said. "She could have been arrested for assault and battery. She could have injured one of the elders, or worse."

"Should I call Caroline?" Jennifer asked. "I mean, does she still want us to plan her wedding?"

"Give her space, Jennifer," Simone advised. "She'll call if she needs us."

Brian, Wanda's husband, called Evelyn with an update. "She's home, resting. Wanda received nine stitches to her forehead, and will need to see a plastic surgeon in a few weeks."

"May I speak with her?" Evelyn asked.

Brian hesitated. Evelyn assumed Wanda was listening, and shaking her head 'no.' "Not right now," he answered sheepishly. "She's sleeping. But I'll tell her to call you when she's up for a chat."

It was another week before Wanda called her mother to give her an update on her condition. "I met with the plastic surgeon, and he said he'll be able to fix the scar across my forehead. If it wasn't for that fat cow, I wouldn't . . . "

"Stop it," Evelyn said sternly. "I don't want to hear anything about that day, except to say that you acted like a child. What happened to you wasn't Caroline's fault. You started the fight."

"I thought you didn't want to talk about it," Wanda reiterated.

"I have to go, Wanda. I hope you feel better," Evelyn said as she hung up the phone. "What did I ever do to that girl to make her so angry?" she uttered out loud to herself.

Forty Two

On New Year's Day 2021, Caroline and Reggie eloped, standing in the gazebo on Main Street in Nyack overlooking ice blocks floating down the Hudson River. They didn't alert anyone of their plans. The officiant came with his wife and adult child, who served as witnesses for the three-minute ceremony.

"This was a much better way of getting married," Reggie said. "I love you so much, Caroline."

"And I love you, Reggie, my husband," Caroline said giggling. "I never thought I'd say those words to anyone."

"To think, it was a crocodile that brought us together," Reggie joked.

After the ceremony, they drove to Adele's home. While standing outside on her front porch, snow covering their hair and clothing, they told her they had married.

Adele was momentarily stunned as she assimilated the news, but she rose to the occasion. "I'm very happy for you both," she said.

"Mom," Caroline said, a smile crossing her face, "there's something else. I'm having a baby."

"Oh, how wonderful!" Adele said, genuinely elated by the news.

"And, we plan to name the baby Devlyn, a combination of my two mother's names: Evelyn and Adele.

Caroline and Reggie waited until the next day to inform their parents of their marriage, and her pregnancy. Reactions were mixed. Reggie's parents, who were not witnesses to Wanda's outburst, were ecstatic to become grandparents. Caroline's mother and father were surprised and happy, yet hurt, that the couple had eloped without the joyous fanfare of a wedding.

Caroline had no intention of calling Wanda with the news, nor had any interest in ever hearing from her again. Wanda's vicious persona was an energy Caroline could permanently live without.

On January eleventh, Jennifer and Mike moved into an extended-stay hotel in Boston, while they searched for a home. A week later, they had their offer accepted on a house in Cambridge, close to the hospital where Mike would be working.

On Saturday, March twentieth, Mike proposed to Jennifer, surprising her with a three-karat diamond engagement ring.

A wedding was planned for September. Goober would be the ring bearer, Simone the matron-of-honor, and the twins, at age two, would be the flower girl and page boy, respectively.

"Mike, I don't have any family to invite to the wedding. My family is Simone, Charlie, the twins, Mrs. Smith and Irene."

"Four adults, and two toddlers?" Mike asked. "That's your whole family?"

"Yes," Jennifer said, feeling a combination of embarrassment and loneliness.

"I have a big family, Jennifer," Mike admitted. He noted her sad demeanor. "But let's keep the guest list small, if that's okay with you. Just my immediate family. We won't invite anyone from the hospital. Once I invite one or two of the doctors, I'd have to invite them all."

"How big is 'big'?" Jennifer asked, referring to his family.

"Well, you've met my two brothers, and my sister. They're all married and have kids. Let's see . . . there's my parents, aunts, uncles, cousins . . ." He stopped counting on his fingers. "Am I upsetting you, Jennifer?"

"No, not at all. Simone and I have worked weddings where the numbers of family members for the bride and groom were not equal. We'll work it out, I'm sure," Jennifer said. "The goal is getting married. It doesn't matter how many people from each side attend the reception." Jennifer stopped and looked up at Mike. "Geez, this is the same guidance I give to brides." She began laughing. "I now have to take my own advice."

"Come on, let's go shopping for furniture," Mike said, adding a lighter note to the moment.

Forty Three

Leslie Marie Morgan decided to join the staff of "I Do." Having a knowledgeable wedding planner, equal in temperament and experience to Jennifer, made the transition go smoothly. Simone did not agree to make Leslie a partner; rather, she assumed a "let's see how things go" attitude. Leslie provided numerous contacts from the New York City metro region, and business boomed once again, as the pandemic seemed to recede and restrictions began to be lifted.

Over the next few months, while Simone needed to pay more attention to the twins, she began working part time. Leslie became the central face of "I Do".

Mrs. Smith and Irene, who were aging gracefully, were finding it difficult keeping up with the toddlers, who were constantly in motion. Simone knew that eventually they no longer would be able to drive the children to nursery school, to after school activities, sporting events and community service activities.

"Simone," Mrs. Smith said one day while the children were playing together, "I think it's time for Irene and I to move closer to Judy. We are both getting up there in age, and we're not able to keep up this pace. Irene needs two knee replacements, and I know I'm going to need to have my hip replaced in the near future. And Judy can use our help now with her newborn."

"I understand," Simone said giving Mrs. Smith a kiss on the cheek. You and Irene have been a tremendous help to Charlie and me during this unprecedented time in our lives." Chuckling, she added, "If you look up Jennifer's husband, he's the head of orthopedics at Boston Hospital. You might get a discount on replacement parts."

"We're thinking of moving in the next six to eight months, Simone. Will you be alright taking care of the little ones without us?"

"Absolutely, Mrs. Smith," Simone said, beaming at the thought of being a stay-at home mom. "I think it's time for me to retire as well. I can't keep up the pace of the wedding planning business . . . traveling coast to coast, and often internationally. Not with these two love-bugs at home," she said smiling at the children. No, Mrs. Smith, I think it's my time, too, to start a new chapter in my life.

Forty Four

Family dynamics were still strained between Wanda and her parents. She purposely hadn't spoken to Caroline in months. Although Evelyn had encouraged both of them to 'make up' neither one was willing to budge.

In February, Brian received a call from a resort hotel in Florida. "Because of the pandemic, we see that you had to cut your stay short the last time you were in our fine state. We'd like to offer you three free nights at our hotel. All you have to do is attend a two-hour presentation on our property, and your visit at our resort will be our gift to you and your family."

Brian took down all the pertinent information and discussed it with Wanda. "It'd be good to get away, after all that's happened this past year. You can finally have your spa day, and I'll take Stella sightseeing. I'm sure they will follow proper pandemic protocol, and we'll be extra careful."

"That sounds wonderful, Brian. Let's do it," Wanda agreed.

"I'll call the sales guy back and make a reservation. He said it's in the Everglades. I've never been to that part of Florida, so it will be a new experience."

Wanda, Brian and Stella arrived at the hotel in Everglades City on Friday, April second. The flight to Florida was uneventful; everyone wore a mask. The weather was very warm, the streets fairly empty, and dining outside was abundant.

The next morning, Wanda rose before Brian and Stella. She left a note: Couldn't sleep. Went for an early morning swim. Back by 9:30.

She headed to the indoor pool. A sign noted that adult swim hours were 7 am – 10 am. Several people were doing laps, and kids played in the smaller children's pool. She wanted to be alone, so she decided to go to the hotel's beach. The area was isolated except for one couple, eating breakfast and engrossed in deep conversation at a far-off picnic table underneath an oversized umbrella. The air was thick with humidity, and the temperature was close to ninety. She settled herself on the hot sand and looked out at the glistening, inviting water. Several 'No Swimming' signs were placed around the perimeter.

Wanda knew it was not safe to enter the water when lifeguards weren't present, and she understood the dangers that lurked in Florida lagoons. But the heat was beginning to mount, and she began sweating. She decided to stand in the shallow end of the pond, and wet her body. She vigorously splashed water on her face, arms and chest. Suddenly and silently, two floating eyeballs stared at her. A muffled scream emanated from her throat as the enormous mouth opened, grabbed Wanda's leg and silently pulled her down underneath the water.

By ten o'clock, Wanda hadn't returned to the room. At ten-thirty, Brian and Stella went down to the concierge desk, inquiring if anyone had seen her.

"No, sir, I haven't seen anyone that fits your wife's

description," the man said. "I arrived an hour ago, and the night shift has left for the day. Let me have your number and I'll call you if I have any information. Maybe she went for breakfast; have you checked the restaurants?"

Brian combed the hotel's breakfast area. The waiter inspected the receipts; no one with their room number had dined in the restaurant that morning. He then headed for the pool. The lifeguard didn't remember seeing anyone matching Wanda's description. The only person in the pool was a man swimming laps.

Brian and Stella raced through the lobby, and out the side door leading to the swimming area. It was nothing more than a man-made beach, with a few tables, an empty lifeguard stand, and a murky-looking pond. There was a couple sitting far off in the distance at a picnic table. Food wrappers and empty coffee cups were piled on the table. Brian asked if they had seen a woman fitting his wife's description.

"Yeah, we saw a woman about an hour ago, when we first got out here. But we didn't see where she went."

"Don't you remember, honey," the woman said, "there was a woman standing by the water? You even thought she must be a foreigner because she ignored the no swimming signs."

"Yeah, now that I think about it, I do remember," he said. "Does your wife speak English?" The young man seemed embarrassed asking Brian this question. "She looked like she ignored the signs and went in the lagoon. But I haven't seen her since."

Brian's face became ashen. He and Stella returned inside the hotel, to the front desk. "Help! Help!" he screamed, as he approached. "I think my wife went swimming in a restricted area."

Staff members gathered. The man got on his radio, and through the static, gave new instructions: "Swimmer in lagoon. I repeat, swimmer in lagoon."

"I saw the no swimming signs," said Brian. But is that because there's no lifeguard on duty?" he asked.

The concierge stared at Brian, then at Stella, and back at Brian. He had no words of comfort or explanation. "Stay here, sir," he demanded.

"I'm coming with you," Brian said. "I want to know where my wife is."

Outside by the lagoon, a small rowboat with two men were out in the middle of the water. One man, with a long harpoon-like pole, pulled something from below. A mixture of water and blood poured from a severed hand. It displayed a gold wedding band that matched Brian's.

"Mommy! Mommy!" screamed Stella. Brian pulled his daughter into his arms, turning her face away from the horror, as the child wept uncontrollably.

"I'm sorry, sir," said the bell captain whispered. "It seems your wife was attacked by a crocodile."

Epilogue

Simone's involvement with "I Do" diminished when she turned her attention to her husband's position at the Grand Hamilton Hotel. She worked from home creating marketing plans and promoting the hotel's innovative renovations and perks. Charlie's new position at the hotel boosted his confidence, as well as with the hotel's Board members. It was his hope the hotel would become a Connecticut destination. He partnered with local companies offering interesting and unusual activities. Guests received discount coupons to local restaurants, wineries, breweries, and team-building activities. Business increased by over fifteen percent in the first six months, with help from Charlie's innovative ideas, and the decrease in COVID numbers.

Jennifer and Mike's wedding was held on a cool September afternoon. Simone's two-year old twins stole the show with their cuteness. Jennifer no longer needed a cane, but did need the support of her dog, Goober. He trotted at Jennifer's heels with two wedding bands loosely held by a ribbon on his collar. He occasionally looked up at her, calming her nerves and anxiety.

The couple settled comfortably into their home in Cambridge, as well as into their marital relationship. Two months after their wedding, Jennifer announced to Simone she was expecting a baby.

Mrs. Virginia Smith and her companion, Irene, moved into an assisted living facility in Brockton, Massachusetts, close to Judy and Harold. The couple welcomed a baby boy they named Harold, Jr. Several months after moving into their apartment, Irene suffered a stroke and passed away. Her death was as devastating to Mrs. Smith as her husband's had been many years ago.

Although she left behind enemies, Wanda's demise was devastating to her parents, her husband and mostly to her daughter, Stella. Much to several family members' surprise, Brian announced his engagement to a woman he claimed he had recently met at work. Suspicions were abundant that they knew each other well before Wanda's accident. "Stella needs a mother," he'd say as an excuse.

Simone reveled in the way life was moving forward for her family, and for those she loved the most. Her business was thriving, at an even pace with Charlie's, although she rarely stepped foot into the "I Do" office these days. Leslie called Simone with updates and for advice. But generally, Leslie ran the business with a sense of ease and professionalism.

Simone's free time was spent with the children and volunteering for local charities. Her knowledge of event planning was invaluable to several non-profit organizations. She often chaired their annual events, giving her great pride and satisfaction.

What life held for Simone's future she didn't know. But, for now, she was enjoying the journey of the new adventures that would be awaiting her at every turn.

www.ingramcontent.com/pod-product-compliance
Lightning Source LLC
Chambersburg PA
CBHW071447170626
46811CB00007B/2501